"How long should I run?" Dana straightened, squaring off as though she was ready for war. "A week? A year? A decade?"

She shook her head and stared at something behind him in the living room. "I hear everything you're saying. Common sense and every ounce of my training say hiding is the best choice. I've preached that to witnesses for years." She sighed, and the lines on her forehead deepened. "But it's not who I am."

The words were soft, but they slammed into his chest, the vocal reminder of her fear, her pain. Of his inability to fix any of this.

"Rich, I may not know a lot of things, including my own name, but I do know not seeking answers will kill me."

It was his turn to flinch. As much as it chilled him from the inside out, she was right.

"I need answers."

"Well, you aren't going alone."

Jodie Bailey writes novels about freedom and the heroes who fight for it. Her novel *Crossfire* won a 2015 RT Reviewers' Choice Best Book Award. She is convinced a camping trip to the beach with her family, a good cup of coffee and a great book can cure all ills. Jodie lives in North Carolina with her husband, her daughter and two dogs.

FATAL IDENTITY

JODIE BAILEY

LOVE INSPIRED SUSPENSE

INSPIRATIONAL ROMANCE

LOVE INSPIRED® SUSPENSE
INSPIRATIONAL ROMANCE

ISBN-13: 978-1-335-40317-9

Recycling programs for this product may not exist in your area.

Fatal Identity

This edition published by arrangement with Harlequin Books S.A.

For questions and comments about the quality of this book, please contact us at CustomerService@Harlequin.com.

Love Inspired
22 Adelaide St. West, 40th Floor
Toronto, Ontario M5H 4E3, Canada
www.Harlequin.com

Printed in U.S.A.

Thine eyes did see my substance, yet being unperfect;
and in thy book all my members were written,
which in continuance were fashioned,
when as yet there was none of them.

How precious also are thy thoughts unto me, O God!
how great is the sum of them!
–Psalm 139:16-17

To Mesu Andrews, Patty Hall, Terri Haynes and Laura Ott...
My "beach retreat sisters" who prayed that "Mary Poppins"
would show up so I could write again.
Thank you.
I love y'all!

ONE

She would not cry. Not today.

Deputy US Marshal Dana Santiago stepped out of a rough wood barn in the middle of nowhere, North Carolina, and stared up at the sky. The stars shone clear and bright after a brief mid-December snow had frosted the ground in fairy dust. Through the wide-open barn doors, the bass of a '70s disco song thumped while laughter overlaid the beat. Weddings didn't usually get to her, but the story behind her teammate Sam Maldonado's trip to the altar with his new bride, Amy, might actually deserve a tear or two. So much pain. So much fear. So much healing.

With the wedding so close to Christmas, when every radio station pumped out nostalgia and every street corner in the tiny town of Mountain Springs was lit with twinkle lights and candy canes…well, even her normally untouchable heart didn't stand a chance.

Maybe she'd even put up a Christmas tree this year.

Dana smiled at the full moon that shone on on Wyatt and Jenna Stephens's property, where Amy Brady and her teammate Sam Maldonado had said their vows earlier. She hadn't had a Christmas tree since she moved out on her own. There was barely time to ship her mom a present, let alone get wrapped up in all of the holiday trappings. Witness Protection didn't take a break on the holidays.

She slipped around the corner of the barn, out of sight of everyone celebrating inside. Rumor had it Amy would be throwing the bouquet soon, and Dana definitely did not want to find herself caught in the single-lady roundup.

The minute Sam proposed to Amy, he'd started assuming the whole world wanted to fall in love, as well. He'd forgotten who he was dealing with. If she wanted to keep advancing in the US Marshals Service, then she had a job to do. Her job sure didn't leave room for romance. Her plane would fly out of Asheville tomorrow morning and she'd be Atlanta-bound, back to work in their team's satellite office by afternoon. Half a week away from her computers was too long. It was time to leave all of the girl talk and dress decisions behind.

In the light that spilled from the barn, parked cars sat in long rows, fading into the darkness. She glanced at her rented sedan toward the middle of the outside row, and her breath caught.

Something moved near the vehicle. A shadowed figure hesitated at the passenger door, then circled to the front and disappeared. He'd probably knelt down to look under the car, likely searching for a hidden key.

Or maybe someone had stepped out to take a phone call and dropped their wallet. This was the downside of her job in Witness Protection—it made her suspicious of every crunching leaf and every partygoer who simply needed a moment of quiet.

Still… Dana glanced at the open barn doors, then back toward the parking area. If someone was out on Wyatt's remote property looking for a quick score, she should alert someone. The wedding reception was in full swing, though, and she really didn't want to drag down the festivities.

Besides, she was a well-trained and competent deputy marshal. If this was a common thief, she could handle the situation. Though her gun remained safely locked away in her room at the bed-and-breakfast, she knew how to inflict serious damage with her hands and feet. She might not be able to recover anything the perp had already stolen, but she could certainly put some fear into him and send him packing.

Slipping into the faint darkness along the perimeter of the makeshift parking lot, Dana eased toward her car as shadows shifted in front of her. If the target left the area around her vehicle, she wanted to know as soon as possible.

She rounded the slight curve in the line and took cover near the front bumper of a blue pickup. Two cars away, only the man's legs and feet were visible beneath her rental vehicle.

She hesitated. He was under her car. This wasn't a petty thief looking for a quick score. He was tampering.

With *her* vehicle.

Either this guy was seriously twisted and had randomly targeted one of the few cars in the lot with out-of-state tags, or he knew who she was. If that was the case, then the situation was a lot more dangerous than—

A strong arm snaked around her waist and jerked

her backward as it lifted her from the ground against a broad chest. A gloved hand clamped over her mouth, grinding leather against her teeth.

She struggled, swung her elbow backward and made contact, but a voice hissed, "You fight, I send my partner into the wedding with guns blazing."

Dana stilled. Sam and Amy had been through enough. The very thought of a massacre at their wedding was intolerable.

She'd bide her time. Sooner or later, her captor would slip up and Dana would find a way to escape him without putting everyone else in danger.

The hand over her mouth jerked her head back and to the side, against a bony shoulder. Pain elicited a feeble cry from her throat as lightning bolts jolted through her neck and down her unnaturally arched spine.

A second man, likely the one who'd been under her car, stepped closer. He tilted his head to study her, his face veiled by shadows, though his dark eyes glittered. He ran one finger down her cheek to her chin then leaned closer. The heat of his breath brushed her skin as his lips swept past her cheek. "*Buenas noches,* Dana Santiago."

Her heart beat faster, and she fought to swallow a flash of panic. He'd used her name. He knew who she was. She was the target.

The angle of her neck kept her immobilized. Dark spots danced before her eyes, and the roar of her pulse pounded in her ears. Her life could not end this way, but her brain fogged and her muscles refused to cooperate. She tried to struggle. Tried to fight. If she lost consciousness, she'd likely never awaken again.

The roar grew louder. The world grew darker. A

voice sounded far away as a presence eased closer. "We have to move quickly, or we'll have more bodies to worry about than hers."

Mountain Springs police officer Alex "Rich" Richardson sat in a white folding chair and glanced around the renovated barn. If he leaned back too far, the rented folding chair would probably give way and dump him on his back. With most of the guests on the dance floor, likely no one would notice, but still…

Besides, he was peopled out for the week. His sweats, his couch and college football were singing their siren song. He crossed his arms over his chest and tried to glance at his watch in a way that wouldn't let the whole place know he was checking the time to see if he'd met his obligatory guest duties. Weddings had never been his favorite thing, and even less so now that—

"Thinking of bolting early on us?" His army buddy Jason Barnes slid into the chair next to his. "The celebration's just getting started."

Rich drummed his fingers on the table. No doubt Jason was in a celebrating mood. He'd been married to Erin for a little less than a year and had announced yesterday that a baby Barnes was on the way. His pal's life was right on track, where he'd always wanted it to be.

Unlike Rich's. This was the third wedding he'd been forced to attend in the past year. First Jason and Erin, then their mutual friends Wyatt and Jenna Stephens, and now this one. Two years ago he hadn't known any of these people except Jason, and now he was not only a guest at their weddings but had somehow managed to have a hand in saving the lives of two of their wives.

Too bad he hadn't been able to save his own fiancée.

Jason stretched out his legs and crossed his arms. "Erin sent me over to see if you'd go find Sam's teammate Dana. She wandered outside, and they want all the single ladies for the bouquet toss."

"She won't come in for that." They'd spent enough time together this week for him to know a bouquet catch wasn't on Dana's bucket list. In fact, she'd probably slipped out and headed back to the B and B where the girls were staying. She was about as much of a social butterfly as he was. They were both social caterpillars who'd stuck close to each other for most of the wedding festivities, chatting about her work with WitSec, his military career and his brand-new job at the police department. Shop. All they'd talked was shop.

It had actually been pretty nice.

Jason looked over his shoulder at the big barn doors. "You're probably right. At least go talk her into coming inside. She's been quiet tonight and needs to have some fun. Sort of like you do."

"You're a laugh riot. Fine. If it will stop you from hounding me…" Rich grabbed his gray blazer from the back of the chair and pulled it on, careful of the twinge that still pinched his shoulder, even after two years. He'd noticed Jason limping earlier, so clearly the cold was hitting them both in their old wounds. Swiping his hands down his jeans, he headed out into the cold, clear mountain night.

Rich scanned the area as the beat of an early-'90s dance jam drowned out the night sounds. The bright stars and the full moon allowed him to see Dana Santiago wasn't anywhere close to the barn.

Wonder where she'd headed? Surely she wouldn't

sneak off without saying goodbye to Sam and Amy. She was friendlier than that, with a full-lipped smile that lit up big brown eyes and—

Really? He'd noticed her eyes were brown? Since when did he notice such stuff?

He was three steps toward the parking lot when activity near the bend in the line of cars quickened his steps. It looked like…trouble.

Two men carried a clearly unconscious woman toward a car whose engine was running. The trunk and both front doors stood open.

The woman's long brown hair swung wildly as they hurried toward the vehicle.

Dana.

This was a snatch-and-grab if he'd ever seen one. Slick. Planned. Targeted. The way those guys were moving, they were experienced.

No time to call for help, not that anyone would hear him over the music. He was on his own. If he could reach them before they knew he was coming, he might be able to intervene.

The man carrying Dana's feet made eye contact with Rich, said something to his partner in what sounded like Spanish, then dropped her feet and made a run for Rich. His shoulder dipped low as though he intended to catch Rich at center mass.

Rich sidestepped at the last second and, with a mighty sideways thrust, caught the man in the shoulder and slammed him into the rear of a pickup. There was a sickening thud as the man's head connected with the bumper. He dropped like a wet rag.

His partner shut the trunk over Dana and raced for

the driver's side of the vehicle, where the door hung open and waiting.

Adrenaline pumping, Rich dived for the open passenger door and made it inside as the driver reached for the gearshift. With all the force he could muster given the tight space, Rich slammed his fist into the driver's jaw with an uppercut.

He sank against the seat, breathing heavily as the other man slumped. Then he looked for a third attacker, but none showed his face. Either these were the only two or anyone else had fled the scene instead of making another run at Dana.

Dana. In the trunk.

Rich turned off the car, grabbed the keys and pressed the trunk release on the key fob. He rushed to the rear of the car. *Lord, let her only be unconscious and not...*

He shook off the rest of the prayer and lifted the lid of the trunk. In the faint light, Dana shifted and scrambled upright, already fighting, then gasped. "Rich." With a sigh that had to empty her lungs, she sank as though her bones had melted.

He reached for her, sliding one arm beneath her knees and the other beneath her back, then hefted her out of the trunk. Her head rested on his shoulder as though she'd been robbed of all fight.

Relief and an adrenaline crash leaked the strength from his muscles. She was alive. "I'm going to get Wyatt, have him arrest these guys and call in backup." As police chief, Wyatt would want to know what had happened on his property ASAP. "Then we'll get you looked at by—"

A scuffing sound whipped him around. The driver

stumbled out of the car and ran for the woods with his buddy on his heels. Rich moved to set Dana down and give chase, but she tightened her grip around his neck and shook her head. "You have to get me out of here, otherwise more will come and someone innocent could get killed."

TWO

"Dana, you have to say something. While I can definitely appreciate the need to run from somebody trying to kidnap you, you can't expect me to go on some wild ride without more intel. Either you start talking, or I hang a U-turn and take you straight back to where this all went down."

Dana stared out the window of Rich's blue pickup and chewed her lower lip as the darkness sped past. He was right, whether she wanted him to be or not. She'd asked him to put his life in danger by being seen with her after the attack, but there had been no other choice.

She couldn't run on her own. There was no telling what those two had done to her vehicle. At best, there was a tracker hooked to the frame.

At worst…it could explode as soon as someone turned the key in the ignition.

Which meant that until someone checked everything out, driving it was out of the question.

"Start talking." Rich's voice was firm, and it brooked no argument.

How could she tell him what was going on when she didn't even know herself? The man knew her name.

He'd targeted her. She had no idea why. If she leaked that bit of intel, every friend she had at WitSec would shut down the wedding reception and start hunting for the reason why. It was bad enough she'd let Rich call the police chief to search for those guys on the down-low.

No, the sooner she put some distance between herself and her friends, the better. "Drop me off at the bed-and-breakfast. I'll change my flight, pick up a ride share to the airport, and then you don't have to worry about—"

"Too late."

She whipped her head toward him. "Too late for what?"

"Too late for you to catch a flight out tonight. Too late for me to drop you off anywhere alone." He flicked a quick glance her way then refocused on the winding road. "Too late for me not to worry."

The words elicited a shiver somewhere in the vicinity of her heart, but she ignored it. "I can take care of myself. I don't need a bodyguard." She'd spent years proving herself in this field where men were perceived to be stronger than women. True, she'd ultimately found her home on the cyber side of WitSec, but she'd done her time pulling security and protecting witnesses. While Rich's Special Forces training probably gave him a slight edge, Dana was as competent as any male deputy marshal. Still, the stab of pain in her neck every time she moved her head screamed how her well-practiced self-defense techniques had failed.

"I have no doubt you're a professional, and I'd never question your abilities." Rich slowed at a stop sign, then turned left. "Having someone watch your back is an asset, not a liability."

"I'm fine. Those men simply saw an opportunity and took it." It was sort of true. They'd taken the opening when she was alone to wrestle her down, but they'd almost definitely been hired to come after her.

Rich didn't need to know that. Because if he did, he'd never let her out of his sight.

"Nice try. Someone tried to kidnap you. Or worse."

"They saw an oppor—"

"That's a great line you keep saying, but do you think I'm an idiot?" It was hard to tell if anger or hurt honed an edge on his words.

No, but she'd kind of hoped he wouldn't be too observant.

Fat chance. The man had been in Special Forces. He probably knew how to observe in his sleep.

"You keep right on saying it was random, but your actions tell me the exact opposite. Two guys grabbed you. You refuse to take your car and insist on taking my truck. You won't let me get help on-site because it might put the entire wedding party in danger."

Oh yeah. She'd said that out loud. Dana dug her teeth into her lip again and waited.

"You forget, I'm unfortunately becoming an expert on pulling security on home turf. Finding out there's a target on your back would be the least surprising thing to happen this year."

He was probably right. When Jenna Stephens had been stalked by her twin sister's would-be murderer, Rich had helped Wyatt stand guard over her. And it had been Rich who provided shelter for Sam and his now-wife, Amy, when her WitSec ID was burned. Seemed he had a way of being where he was needed most.

Dana didn't want to need him.

Rich slowed to pull onto a winding road on the side of a mountain. It didn't look like the route to the B and B, but she hadn't been this way in the dark before. "They weren't trying to kidnap me. They were trying to kill me."

Rich slammed on the brakes, the back end of the truck fishtailing slightly. "There's a whole lot more you need to be telling me."

"I'm sorry that I put you in the middle of this."

He sliced the air with his hand then leaned across her, popped the glove compartment open and pulled out a pistol. He leaned to the side and anchored the holster to his belt. "The problem isn't you got me involved. The problem is you think someone wants you dead. Why?"

"I don't know."

"A little truth, please?"

Dana sighed. He'd never stop asking. But if she was in his shoes, neither would she. "They knew my name."

Rich scrubbed the back of his neck. "That changes everything. You're a deputy marshal, along with several key people at the wedding. The reception could be a target."

"No." Dana shook her head. "They headed for me. For my vehicle. This isn't about my team, or they'd have gone straight for them. It's personal."

The silence deepened as he eyed her, probably considering his next move.

The trill of his phone over Bluetooth made Dana jump.

Rich glanced at the radio then pulled to the side of

the road. "Wyatt." He punched a button on the steering wheel. "You're on speaker."

"We made a quick search for your bad guys, but we didn't find anything. Preliminary run of the plates on the car says it was reported stolen in Asheville earlier today. Once the reception breaks up, I'll have someone tow it and the department will process it. No sense disrupting Sam and Amy's big day, but I've got a few extra officers keeping an eye on things just in case."

Dana kept her gaze away from Rich as she leaned closer to the mic on his side of the truck. "Have someone sweep my rental car before they move it. One of the guys was underneath."

Rich muttered something under his breath.

"Are you kidding me?" Wyatt sounded frustrated, and she couldn't blame him. As Mountain Springs' newest police chief, he knew this wasn't something they could ignore. "Are you thinking a bomb?"

"More likely a tracker."

"Dana, what's going on here? There are eighteen things wrong with how this is going down. I've got two criminals on the loose, a rental car that's been tampered with and a stolen vehicle. We haven't even begun talking about the fact someone attacked a deputy US marshal on my private property. You need to get back here. Now."

Dana shook her head. "Give me some time to sort this out and then I'll talk to you. Let Sam and Amy have their night." They deserved it. Dana heading anywhere near the wedding would be problematic if those men were still skulking around.

"Where are we going?"

"I'm taking her to my place for the rest of the night. It's less obvious than the police station and so isolated no one should be able to find her."

"No!" Dana snapped. If they were being followed, taking her to his place would mount a target in the center of his forehead.

"Do you want to be at the B and B with the rest of the wedding party if those guys come looking?"

True. "Take me to a hotel." She wouldn't be responsible for another person's death. It would kill her.

Wyatt's voice broke in. "I agree. Your place is safer. I'll be there in an hour to get her statement, and we can decide what to do from there." He cut the call.

"I am not taking you to a hotel." Rich rested his hand along the back of the seat, checked the road behind them and shifted the truck into gear. "You'll be safer at my place."

"I need some of my stuff."

"Absolutely not."

"I'm not dumb enough to grab anything electronic. My phone is at the barn with my purse, which I'll need to fly home tomorrow. But I do want different clothes." She extended her leg to display a rip in her skirt. "At least let me grab clean jeans."

"They knew your car. They knew you'd be at the wedding. That tells me they definitely know where you're staying. If I were them and you were my mission? I'd hightail it straight to the B and B and wait for you to show up. It's tactical skills 101, and if you were thinking straight, you'd know it." He handed her his phone. "Text Wyatt that you need your ID. Have him get an officer to take your belongings to the station.

I have some of Am—" He cleared his throat. "I've got some old clothes at the house that might fit you."

Dana furrowed her brow but said nothing. She couldn't go back to the B and B. He was right—she wasn't thinking straight.

And with Wyatt and Rich on one side and two hired guns on the other, she was also trapped.

While Rich walked Wyatt to the door, Dana slouched against the leather couch cushion, stretched her legs and wrapped her arms over her eyes. The only good thing to say about the past two hours was she'd finally been able to change out of her ripped skirt and a shirt that hadn't been comfortable even when she put it on earlier in the afternoon. The borrowed jeans were a little loose, but the Auburn University sweatshirt was the next best thing to a warm hug. Whoever these clothes belonged to, they were all about comfort.

Comfort was what she needed right about now. Between the attack and walking a tightrope of answers to Wyatt's questions, she was as wrung out as an old dishrag. If everyone would leave her alone, she could sleep right here.

Rich's footsteps thudded across the hardwood, and the leather of the love seat across the coffee table from her creaked. "Doing okay?"

The question was softer than his usual all-business tone, and something about the timbre of it brought tears to the corners of her eyes. Dana swallowed hard. No. Those men did not get to make her cry. She cleared her throat. "I'm fine."

"Sure you are."

Dana pulled her arms apart an inch and peeked between them. Rich sat in a position almost identical to hers, legs outstretched but with his arms along the back of the love seat, making his shoulders appear even broader than usual. He looked relaxed, but she'd worked too many protection details to miss his tense signals. His posture was tight, like a cat ready to pounce. While his head was leaned back on the couch and his gaze fixed on the wood-beamed ceiling, the tilt of his chin said he was tuned in for sounds that had nothing to do with her answer to his question. Even though Wyatt had posted officers nearby, Alex Richardson wasn't the kind of guy to relax.

This was more than military and police training, though. The way he talked, the way he acted… It ran deeper than duty. Too bad she didn't know him well enough to ask what made him tick. She could use a conversation not directly focused on her.

Dana dropped her hands to her sides and glanced around the room. The house was larger than she'd expected, with exterior walls made of polished logs and interior walls painted white. The hardwood floors nearly matched the logs, but braided rugs broke up the monochrome effect. In the corner near the fireplace, a massive tree held court, decorated with old-fashioned bulb lights and ornaments shaped like fish, birds and other outdoorsy kinds of things.

A massive TV dominated the space over the fireplace, while fly-fishing rods and outdoor prints decorated the walls. Several seating areas of leather couches and chairs gathered around the room, and a dining room table anchored the other side of the open kitchen. The whole space was masculine yet meticulously planned and designed. "This is your house?"

"I live here."

Interesting answer. Dana eyed the upstairs balcony over the kitchen. Several closed doors to what were probably bedrooms led off the entry. "So whose house is it?"

"It's mine."

Dana shifted her gaze to the man across from her. "I don't like riddles."

"I'm not trying to be one." He leaned farther into the sofa and laced his fingers behind his head. "I own the house. I live in the house. But it's not necessarily for me."

"Riddles."

He flashed a smile that flew away as quickly as it landed. "A few years ago, after an incident overseas, the army stationed me and my team at Camp McGee as instructors. After some other events happened..." He took a deep breath and exhaled slowly, still staring at the ceiling instead of looking at her. "Well, a couple of us attended an outdoor retreat in Colorado. They offered therapy to wounded warriors and those suffering from PTSD. I got to thinking I could see myself doing the same thing for others.

"I grew up not too far from here, spent my childhood years fishing and hunting, so I bought half of the side of the mountain. Somebody built the house to be a bed-and-breakfast, but I got a deal when the property went into foreclosure. It makes a good base camp, and the TLC it required kept me busy whipping it back into livable shape." He shrugged and sat up, aiming his gaze at the fireplace behind her. "So yeah, it's mine, but it also will eventually belong to the nonprofit."

"You decorated it?" Because if he did, he could come down to Atlanta and do something about her apartment. She'd lived there for five years, but the walls were still bare. Who had time to fuss with pictures and knickknacks?

"You think I couldn't? Are you stereotyping? Implying that all guys have bad taste?" For the first time, real amusement sparked in his eyes.

Boy, did it change everything about him. It made him human, softer...and downright gorgeous. Not in the classic sense. More in a rough-around-the-edges, scruffy kind of way.

Nope. Dana crossed her arms over her eyes again. She couldn't go down that road. Not with a job that demanded all her time and energy. "It's a really nice place."

"If you're tired, you can take your pick of rooms upstairs. They're not decorated, but there's a bed in each one. You're probably ready to hit the rack."

It was weird, him playing host. They'd chatted over the past few days, but it had all been surface topics and career stories. Hanging out at his house seemed to catapult them into the kind of friendship she had with Sam and her other teammate, Isaac. Those partnerships had taken years to build. No way could she have camaraderie with this guy so quickly.

Not that it mattered. There wouldn't be a lot of sleep happening for her tonight, even though she'd been entertaining thoughts of dropping where she sat. "I'm good, but if you had some coffee, I could definitely go for the biggest mug you've got."

"Not a problem." The couch creaked again as Rich stood. "I don't keep girly-flavored creamer around, though."

"Girly?" Dana dropped her hands from her eyes and sat up. She watched Rich head for the open kitchen, where he filled the coffeepot at the brass-and-ceramic sink. City girl that she was, she could get used to the kind of rustic beauty this upscale cabin offered. It was quiet and would be peaceful if she didn't keep picturing killers lurking in the dark woods outside. "I drink it black. And since when is creamer only for girls? Now who's stereotyping?"

"I've never used it."

"And you are the only man in the whole wide world." She sat up taller and stretched her arms wide, the sleeves of the sweatshirt sliding to her elbows.

Man, she could fall in love with this outfit. The sweatshirt was obviously his. When she moved, it carried the faint whiff of whatever mysterious scent guys seemed to have. But the jeans? These were perfectly worn women's jeans. "Speaking of girly stuff…why do you have a woman's clothes at your house?"

"What?"

Yeah, he might be acting like he didn't hear her, but the way those broad shoulders stiffened ever so slightly said otherwise. Why would a question about clothes make him bristle? Come to think of it, he hadn't even looked her in the eye since he handed over the jeans and sweatshirt before Wyatt arrived.

Interesting.

Peeling herself from the couch, Dana padded across the hardwood to the bar separating the kitchen from the living area. She leaned on her elbows and planted her toes, stretching her battle-weary legs. "I think you heard the question."

"I think I didn't answer." The words weren't angry. They were flat. Empty of all emotion.

Dana slid onto a wooden stool and leaned her elbows on the bar, resting her chin on her laced fingers. While Rich loaded up the coffee maker, his movements precise and measured, she simply waited. Something in her gut said not to push. He'd speak when he was ready.

Maybe.

After he pressed the start button, Rich reached above the machine and grabbed two thick pottery mugs. When he turned and set them on the counter by the bar, his eyes caught hers for the first time since she'd changed clothes.

He swallowed so hard his Adam's apple dropped. Even though something haunted flickered across his expression, he didn't look away. Neither did Dana. Those stormy eyes trapped her, caught her up and swept her into the pain hidden there. "I'm sorry." The words escaped before her good sense could stop them.

Rich blinked and turned away, apparently watching the coffee drip into the pot. "For what?"

"For whatever happened to make you look like you just looked."

He froze. His back and shoulders were a solid line. The muscles in his neck tensed. For a long time, he said nothing, but then his chin lifted ever so slightly. "Sweatshirt's mine. Jeans belonged to my fiancée. Her parents asked me to drop them off at a charity, but I never did."

Parents. Charity. Past tense. Something really bad

must have occurred. "What happened?" Her voice fell to a whisper. This was sacred space, although she had no idea why.

Rich sniffed. "She was murdered." He turned, and his gray gaze pinned hers. "Because of me."

THREE

A flicker of questions and grief raced across Dana's face, but she buried it almost as quickly as it surfaced. Clearly, her training had taught her how to hide emotions well.

Yeah, well, he'd had training, too. Rich schooled his face to remain impassive. Letting her drag him into a personal conversation had been his *second* mistake. He never talked about Amber. Not to anybody, let alone to a woman he barely knew.

Looking directly at her had been his *first* mistake. After Amber died, her parents had taken most of her personal effects with them, and he'd kept a couple of mementos that were special to him. They'd asked him to drop two bags of clothes off at the women's shelter in Asheville, but he'd kept a few pairs of blue jeans and sweatpants in case any women ever came to the retreat and needed a change of clothes after a day on the river. It had seemed like a smart move. Loaning them to Dana so she would be comfortable was the decent thing to do.

But it wasn't someone else wearing Amber's clothes that bothered him. That part he could handle. What he hadn't been prepared for was seeing his sweatshirt on Dana. It was weirdly intimate. The only woman who'd ever worn his jacket or sweatshirt before was Amber, and then only a handful times.

That had been natural. She'd been cold, and he was all protective instincts and gentlemanly gestures thanks to his mother…

He'd always thought it made Amber look small and cute and vulnerable, considering how much bigger he was than her.

His sweatshirt had the same effect on Dana Santiago, making her appear in need of protection, like Amber had been.

He'd failed Amber.

And he couldn't fail another woman the way he nearly had tonight.

A woman who was currently speaking to him.

Rich shook his head, hoping to kick out some of the dusty cobwebs of memory. "I'm sorry. What?"

"How did she die because of you?" Dana was studying him as if she was trying to read his thoughts.

The coffee maker beeped, and he snagged her mug from the counter then turned away. After pouring her a cup, he set it before her. Then he grabbed his mug. With his back to her, he poured his coffee slowly, watching the rich liquid fill the mug that Wyatt's wife, Jenna, had made for him last year.

How was Amber's death because of him?

"Because I was arrogant." When the threats came to the wives and girlfriends of the men in his unit, Amber hadn't wanted to move on base, where she'd be more protected. At the time, he couldn't blame her. Some of the wives took shelter in a hotel on post, staying confined to their rooms out of fear of the killer. Amber had been adamant she wouldn't live in a prison.

"I thought I could protect her better than anyone else. When…when she was threatened, instead of moving her to safety on base, I let her stay in the spare room at my apartment." A deadly mistake. When Amber insisted she keep her regular routine, he'd followed along, convinced someone as well trained as he was wouldn't miss the fatal blow if it came her way.

But he had. And Amber had died in his arms.

Worse, the killer had been someone they both knew and trusted. Someone he'd never suspected, not even for one moment.

He'd missed *everything*. While he'd grieved Amber and forced himself to carry on with his life, he lay awake far too often wrestling with the little things he could have done differently.

"Good coffee. What kind is it?" From the bar, Dana's voice shifted to a lighter tone.

Guess she'd picked up he wasn't going to divulge anything else. He actually managed to round up a half chuckle. "Don't go thinking you're going to find coffee like that in Atlanta. The coffee shop owner in Mountain Springs roasts her own in small batches. Her name's Shannon. She's good people." Good people he'd gone out with a time or two last year. In the end, he'd driven himself insane watching the crowd around her for threats. When she of the dyed purple hair had deemed him too serious for her tastes, they'd agreed to remain friends.

Dana cleared her throat. "Coffee mug is nice, too. Good and heavy. Holds a lot."

The small talk was killing him, but if he didn't

follow along, she might go back to her original line of questioning. Either way, it was going to be a long night. Steeling himself against the sight of her, he turned so she at least wouldn't be talking to his back. "Jenna made them. She made all of the dishes here, a set of twenty-eight."

"Nice. That will be a real draw for—"

Rich's phone buzzed on the polished butcher block counter. He slid it closer and glanced at the screen.

Wyatt. Adams saw movement heading toward your location from road. Two men. Hunker down. Could be more. On my way.

He pocketed the device. His jaw clenched until his head ached.

Dana must have noticed. Setting her coffee mug on the counter, she slid off the bar stool, her back ramrod straight. She was more alert than she'd been for the past two hours. Clearly the woman was a fighter. "What?"

"Someone's headed this way. It's about a mile to the road through thick woods, so it will take time for them to get here, but that doesn't mean we're not in danger." He rounded the counter and laid a hand on her back, ushering her toward the room where he kept the gun safe. "You have a preference in sidearms?"

She didn't flinch. "I usually carry a Glock 23."

"I've got close enough to that. We can take cover in—"

A soft pop. The lights flickered once, then the house fell into darkness.

Dana's breath caught in midinhale. One socked foot slipped forward, and she teetered back against Rich's chest.

He wrapped an arm around her waist and helped her regain her balance. "You good?"

"Yeah." She twisted free, trying to get her bearings, but it was too dark and she had no idea of the house's layout. She was helpless to save herself.

And she *hated* it. She wasn't a weak woman, but nobody would know based on her circumstances.

Rich slipped past her. "Grab the back of my shirt. The gun safe is in a room behind the laundry area. Center of the house. No windows. Only one door. Best defendable position we've got."

Dana obeyed, wrapping her fingers into his dress shirt, his back warm and oddly comforting through the thin material. As her eyes adjusted, the shape of him grew clearer in the dim moonlight filtering through the windows onto the floor in cold pools. The way he held his arm, it was obvious he'd drawn his sidearm and held it at the ready. "Hope you can get the safe combination in the dark." She felt exposed without a weapon, even though her companion was more than capable.

"I've got it covered. Just trust me."

What other choice did she have? Rich might be a virtual stranger, but Sam had trusted him to protect Amy, so he'd earned Dana's respect. Still, it went against everything inside her to relinquish control. She was the one who protected others, who put herself between them and harm's way.

This was all backward.

With a breath she hoped would calm her aching lungs and infuse some oxygen to her muddled brain, Dana nodded then glanced through the open door to her right as they passed. Moonlight poured into what appeared to be a small office.

A shadow drifted past the window.

Her pulse throbbed in her throat. "Rich…"

"I saw it." Ducking around a corner, he stepped through a door and closed it.

Immediately, the room plunged into thick darkness. The familiar scent of laundry detergent and bleach tickled Dana's nose. In a crazy way, the smell was almost comforting. Normalcy in the middle of chaos. "You use the same detergent as me."

"Weird observation, but okay. Whatever gets you through this." In the darkness, they passed through a second door, and Rich shut it behind them. "You can let go now."

Dana released his shirt and her breath at the same time, then flexed her fingers. She'd been holding on to him tighter than she'd realized. "This your safe room?"

Dim light illuminated the space with a faint blue glow as Rich unlocked his cell phone and sent a text, probably alerting Wyatt to their location so officers would be able to find them. "There's a safe, but that's coincidence. I don't have a panic room, although lately…" The pale glow sank his face into shadows, making him look more serious, almost menacing.

At least the menace was aimed at whoever stalked her.

He passed the phone to her. "Hold it where I can see the safe."

She obeyed, and he twirled the combination then pulled the door open. He slid the clip into place and passed her the semiautomatic, grip first. "Thirteen rounds in the magazine." He hesitated, then handed her a second clip.

Twenty-six rounds. This was war. If she had to pull the trigger twenty-six times…

It would be the shootout to end all shootouts.

The odds of dying grew with each passing moment.

"Take a knee by the safe, facing the door. I'll position myself to the left of the door. If someone comes through, I'll stay left and out of your line of fire. I'll shoot first. You're on deck if I miss."

"Got it." Slipping the spare clip into her hip pocket, Dana went to one knee. If anyone came through the door…

Well, if anyone entered, she'd put into practice training she never wanted to use. Pulling the trigger on another human being was the one thing she'd managed to avoid her entire career. The thought conjured up the image of a recurring nightmare she'd had since she was a child. A man, pistol in hand, standing over a second man…

Dana shuddered away the bloodied vision as Rich locked his phone. Total darkness filled their small space. With her sight eliminated, her hearing amped.

Rich's breathing shifted, and he moved to the left. He was in position.

Dana managed her own breaths. *In, two, three… Out, two, three.*

A crash. Glass shattered.

Dana's breath hitched.

"Not good," Rich muttered.

No, it wasn't. Whoever was coming in didn't care if they were detected. Either they were incredibly stupid, which made them dangerous, or they were confident in their superior firepower, which made them an even bigger threat.

Two thuds came from the direction of the living area. Two people dropping to the floor through the window. Two on two. They could—

A third thud. Then a fourth.

Dana's grip on the gun tightened, and she could practically feel Rich tense. Four assassins in the house. Who knew how many outside. They were outnumbered and likely outgunned.

"Come on, Wyatt." Rich's mutter of frustration was probably one he'd meant to keep inside, but Dana could understand. They had no idea what they faced on the other side of the door. In the darkness, fighting back would be tough. Cross fire could be a bigger threat than hired guns.

Footsteps creaked on hardwood, moving in so many directions throughout the house that they layered over each other. Dana couldn't keep track. Pulse pounding, she shifted and anchored her position to steady herself.

Someone called out in Spanish, directing the crew, sending two of them upstairs.

One set of footsteps plodded closer, the creaking hardwood floor alerting them to the man's position. He hesitated outside the laundry room door. A slight swish. He'd entered and was only feet away.

Light swept under the doorway of Dana and Rich's hideaway.

A flashlight.

She pulled in a deep breath, held it, then released it. Aim at the beam.

Silence reigned in the room for a moment, then there was a rustle. A click. The light grew brighter.

Dana raised her weapon and slipped her finger to the trigger.

FOUR

Rich holstered his pistol.

If they needed firepower, Dana was armed and he'd trust her training.

But if he could catch this guy as he entered, get him in a sleeper hold and subdue him, then his partners would be none the wiser.

Three to two.

With two upstairs and only one down, it might be possible to pick them each off without firing a shot.

The door edged open. A flashlight beam swept the room from left to right, illuminating Dana.

There was a sharp inhale from their stalker as he prepared to announce his find, but Rich was faster. Before the man could exhale a warning, Rich wrapped his arm around the perp's neck and jerked him closer. Flexing his arm to tighten the pressure against the man's jugular veins, he held on with all his might as the guy struggled and clawed, then slowly went limp.

Rich's breath almost left him, too. He lowered the man to the ground, then grabbed the flashlight and aimed it at the shelf above the safe. "Duct tape. Cover his mouth first, then secure him. I'm heading out. You stay here. I don't want you caught in the cross fire if it goes south."

Dana reached for the duct tape. "I'm not hunkering down like a groundhog who's seen his shadow."

"Not arguing," Rich hissed. "In the dark, can't tell who's who. Both of us out there is asking for trouble."

In answer, she knelt and ripped a strip of duct tape.

Rich killed the flashlight then pulled out his phone to pass intel to Wyatt. Four men. Two up. One down. One subdued. Dana with gun safe. I'm moving out. He slipped through the door into the laundry room. Dana was a smart woman. His explanation should be enough to make her stay put.

Though he fully acknowledged that, in her shoes, he'd chafe at standing still, too.

Faint moonlight illuminated the hallway. Rich stopped at the threshold. Doors opened and closed upstairs, but there was silence down here. Had he made enough racket taking out their first target to alert the second to their whereabouts?

Where was Wyatt? The police chief was smart enough not to respond and set Rich's phone abuzz, but not having intel made him a little uncertain. Did he take on the bad guys alone and risk getting himself or Dana hurt? Or did he wait an extra thirty seconds and hope the cavalry kicked down the doors?

The floor at the head of the hallway near the living room creaked.

Okay, then. Guess the choice was made. He steeled himself for another confrontation. This time, the footsteps were almost silent, stealthy, as though the man knew Rich lay in wait. Only the occasional creak gave him away.

Closer…closer…

A double crash. A curse in Spanish.

Chaos broke loose in the house.

Flashlight beams from every direction. Shouts of "Police!" Pounding feet reverberating throughout the house.

Moments later, members of the Mountain Springs PD rushed in through the front and back doors.

The man in the hallway ran for the office, and Rich itched to pursue, but he didn't want to be mistaken for a bad guy and get himself shot.

Glass shattered.

"Got a runner!" More men ran for the exits.

A flashlight and a figure appeared in the doorway, the beam aimed at the floor. "Rich. You okay?"

He sank against the wall at the sound of Wyatt's voice and exhaled in relief. "Am now."

"Hang tight until I can get your generator up and running. We want to do a sweep with some lights on before we set you two loose."

Two more flashlight beams bobbed closer up the hall, and the police chief directed the officers to take custody of Dana's prisoner before he walked toward the back door.

Dana followed the officers as they escorted their suspect out. She stopped beside Rich. "I'm keeping your pistol until I get mine back."

"Ammo, too?"

"Ammo, too."

"With the police presence here now, I'm pretty sure our new friends are done wreaking havoc for one night."

Her elbow brushed his as she shifted, and her shadowy form leaned against the washing machine. "Yeah? Well, you also thought we'd be safe here in the first place. Pretty gutsy on their part, trying to get the drop on a federal agent and a former soldier turned local LEO."

"Yeah. Gutsy." That's what had him worried. Either there was a huge contingent tasked with taking Dana Santiago down, or someone had put a pretty hefty bounty on her head. Hefty enough to bring the local thugs out of their holes. "Say, who do you think is—"

A low hum drifted in from outside, echoed by a fainter one from the kitchen, and the lights snapped on. Rich sagged against the door, the remaining tension easing from his shoulders. At least now they could dispel the shadows that might hide another assailant.

He itched to help with the search of his own house, but Wyatt had ordered him to stay put, so he'd comply, even though he disagreed with the order. The army bred arguing with authority figures right out of a man.

"So we're stuck here while everyone else does the heavy lifting?" Dana planted her palms on the dryer and hefted herself up to sit on the top. She arched an eyebrow with a half smile. "Got a deck of cards handy?"

Who was this woman? Two attempts on her life in as many hours, and she was cracking jokes about boredom? "Afraid not. But I'll be sure to put some in the gun safe for next time."

The amused glint in her eye dimmed. "There had better not be a next time. With at least one of them in custody, hopefully we'll get the answers we need and can shut this thing down."

Footsteps seemed to fill his entire house and the

space between them. Doors opened and closed, followed by random shouts of "Clear!" as rooms were checked and likely double-checked.

Dana slid off the dryer and stood in the doorway beside him, although there wasn't much to see from their vantage point. Like him, it probably made her feel better to pretend to do something other than sit.

While she wasn't touching him, she was close enough for him to catch the scent of whatever soap or lotion she used. Amber had always smelled like flowers, some stuff from that place at the mall.

Now the faint scent of coconut, almost like sunscreen, floated around him. Reminded him of summer trips to the beach and the vague sense of happiness that permeated those memories.

Happiness? Right. The one thing in life that never lasted. It wasn't an emotion to trust. When it got jerked out from under you, there was no way to find it again.

He backed away and turned toward the fridge in the corner of the laundry room. "Thirsty?"

"Hmm?" She kept her eyes on the door. "Um… no, thanks."

Rich popped the lid on a water bottle and leaned against the refrigerator, watching the way her dark hair waved to a spot between her shoulder blades. So different than Amber's dark blond ponytail.

So different from Amber in every way.

He chugged the water and crushed the bottle. Why was he even comparing the two? They were two different women who held completely different roles in his life. There was no comparing a fiancée to a stranger. None.

Tossing the bottle into the trash can by the dryer,

he crossed his arms over his chest and stared at the wall. No comparison at all.

Why did it feel like she'd already been in this position once before?

Dana planted her feet on the hardwood floor and fought to stay upright on couch cushions that tempted her exhausted mind and body to sleep. Now wasn't the time for rest. Despite her assertions earlier, she was pretty sure this was nowhere near over.

Then again, half of the Mountain Springs Police Department stood watch outside. Chief Wyatt Stephens stood by the TV, still wearing the jeans and button-down shirt he'd had on at the wedding. The tie was gone now, though. He eyed her as though he thought she had all the answers to tonight's mysteries hidden in her brain.

Well, she didn't. All she knew for sure, particularly now that Rich's house had become a target, was that she was the one in the crosshairs.

After a silence that stretched past eternity, Wyatt scrubbed his hand along the back of his neck and exhaled slowly. "I can't believe we're doing this again." He turned to look at Rich, who stood by the front window, staring into the darkness.

"It can't become a way of life, for sure."

They didn't have to talk in code. She knew the dangerous past of Mountain Springs. Wyatt's wife, Jenna, had been hunted down by a human trafficker who thought she was her twin sister. Wyatt had been an officer in the police department then. He'd protected Jenna, and Rich had stepped in as backup. She was a little less clear about what had happened to Jason and

Erin Barnes, but somehow Rich had been involved. As for Jenna's sister, Amy, she and Rich had both been separately involved in the mission.

But they were civilians. She was a marshal. Dana stood, drawing the attention of both men. "You guys remember who I am, right? I'm the one who helped take down Amy's would-be killer. I'm the one who worked with Sam to keep her safe. I'm—"

"You're the one who has a target in the middle of her forehead." From the kitchen her team leader, Isaiah Evans, spoke. Wyatt had contacted him, and he'd arrived shortly after the house was cleared.

Other than a check on her status when he first came in, Isaiah had leaned against the kitchen counter taking in the scene, probably evaluating Wyatt and Rich. It was what he did. He might be six foot three and built like a linebacker, but his superpower was the observational skills locked in his brain.

She glanced over her shoulder at the man who sometimes felt more like a brother than a team leader. "Nobody asked you."

With a shrug, he hefted his coffee and took a sip without looking away from her.

Dana rolled her eyes and made a face, then decided that ran counter to the point she was trying to make. She was competent. She could take care of herself. She—

Rich and Wyatt watched as though deciding whether to send her to her room without dessert.

Without commenting, Rich turned to the window, but a smile ghosted his face.

So, they'd seen her little-kid side. Everybody had one. "It's not the first time I've been in the cross fire.

Before I went into the cyber side of the house, I protected witnesses in situations just like this."

"That's the problem." Wyatt put on a no-nonsense police chief voice. "You're not in the cross fire. You're in the direct line of fire."

"Don't be stubborn, Santiago." Isaiah appeared at her elbow then dropped into the chair that angled to the couch. "We know you're a rock star. You have nothing to prove. I've seen you in action on both sides of the house, with boots on the ground and behind a computer screen. You're good, but you're not faster than a bullet."

As much as she wanted to sink to the sofa and close her eyes and ears, she stood her ground. "Precisely. I'm good at what I do, and I'm supposed to fly out in a few hours to go back to doing it." She looked at Isaiah. "We have to get to Atlanta. Our entire team went off duty to be at this wedding. Sam's gone for two weeks on his honeymoon…"

Sam. Wedding. Her eyes widened, and she leaned closer. "Tell me you kept your mouth shut and he's halfway down the mountain to wherever he and Amy were supposed to stay tonight." If she was responsible for wrecking his honeymoon, she'd never forgive herself.

Isaiah dismissed her concerns with a wave. "I didn't even know anything until the reception had already wound down and Rich called. Sam and Amy took off around midnight in a classic 'Vette with tin cans trailing. They'll be safely on a plane at first light."

This time she did sink into the sofa. "Good. He's got too strong a sense of duty. If he thought one of us was in trouble, he'd be here in a heartbeat."

Isaiah nodded. "Good thing there's no cell reception where those two are going, huh?"

"Look who's talking." Rich finally left the window and walked over to stand behind Isaiah's chair. "I think the strong-sense-of-duty thing rubbed off on Dana."

"She was born with it." Isaiah scoffed. "What's the plan?"

"There's no plan." They didn't get to sit here and act like she was invisible, like she couldn't handle this. "As I said, tomorrow morning, I get on a plane to Atlanta. I don't think there's another way to tell you guys I have a job to do. We have witnesses in the system. Agents in the field. I'm the cyber investigator for the entire region. I can't be away from my duties any longer."

"You're not indispensable." Isaiah sliced the air with his hand then sat back and stared at the dark TV screen.

Dana bit her tongue to keep from saying something she'd regret. But he was wrong. The job needed her, and she needed the job. She *was* the job. Her lab was her design, and she'd developed the proprietary software the team used to trace threats. Cyber wouldn't look the same without her.

That wasn't arrogance. It was straight fact. "I need to work." She'd lose her mind sitting around with nothing to do. "It's WitSec. We're locked tight. I'm safer on the job than anywhere else."

"It's true." At least Isaiah had taken her side this time.

"Well, I don't like it." Wyatt watched her as though contemplating how to handle a problem like Dana.

Well, *she'd* had enough. This was her life. Her job.

Her choice. "Seems to me you don't get a lot of say in it."

"Also true." Isaiah again.

Maybe she'd forgive him for his earlier comments after all.

"Y'all realize the testosterone in this room is out of control, right?" She stood and turned to Wyatt. It was high time she took back the reins of her life. "Since this place is better guarded than Fort Knox and they already know where to find me, I'd like my suitcase from the B and B, please." She pivoted and looked at Rich. "My flight leaves at nine. I'll need a ride to the airport. Now, I'd like to take you up on that offer of a place to sleep." Because frustrated ire wasn't going to keep her on her feet much longer.

"We'll leave at seven." Rich seemed to get she was done. He waved an arm at the stairs. "Pick a room."

With a nod to the men, Dana headed for the stairs, praying all the way her legs wouldn't give out as exhaustion kicked in. Being rude wasn't her usual stance, but at least she'd regained control of the situation.

Even though the war had only just begun.

FIVE

"So you wrangled your way into coming with me. Where exactly do you plan to stay?" Dana refused to look at Rich as he climbed out of her car. She slammed the door of the Charger so hard the sound echoed through her apartment building's parking garage.

Apparently, asserting her independence then heading off for a couple of hours of restless sleep the night before was the worst thing she could have done. Not only was she twice as cranky as before, but she'd somehow inherited a bodyguard after she finally managed to fall asleep. In the short time she'd been out, the trio downstairs had managed to set a plan into place and to secure Rich a plane ticket. It seemed Isaiah believed she'd be safer with a traveling companion. While he hadn't ordered her to accept it, his firm tone when he'd informed her had been more than direct.

She snatched her suitcase from the trunk and contemplated shutting Rich's gear inside. Because he'd packed both of their weapons secured in his duffel bag, they'd had to wait for his luggage at baggage claim. If she locked his stuff away, hers would be right beside it.

Rich shut his door with a bit less authority than

Dana had, then joined her. He hefted his duffel bag onto his shoulder then closed the trunk. "I think the better question is where do *you* plan to stay?"

She stopped and stared at the building's gray metal doors. How was that even a question? "In my apartment?" Why did she act like he held the answer?

It was bad enough he'd hauled a duffel bag out of the bed of his pickup at the airport and announced Wyatt and Isaiah had decided he should travel with her. For one thing, she didn't need a babysitter. For another, if Isaiah was so worried, he could have changed his and his wife's tickets to fly with Dana. They hadn't needed to pull Rich from his job in the police department to tag along with her. She worked for WitSec. Even if she couldn't take care of herself, she was surrounded by plenty of people who could.

"I'm staying in my apartment. You're not stopping me." Dana started walking again, her pace brisk.

Rich's footfalls followed on her heels.

Right now, she had so many words for Isaiah… She punched the button on the elevator and reached for her phone, then glanced at her watch instead. His flight left Asheville in an hour, and he was likely already at the gate with his cell phone turned off. His wife, Trina, hated to fly, so she'd have his full attention.

It was probably best not to make too much noise about Rich's presence, though. Isaiah could always order her to relocate to their secured office. Sleeping on a cot for an undetermined amount of time appealed even less than having a bodyguard.

Rich followed her into the building and down the short hallway to the elevator. She glanced over at his single duffel bag. "You're not staying with me."

"Relax." His voice sounded as tired as she felt.

Maybe she should let up on him a little. He hadn't asked for any of this. If he'd spent the night discussing logistics with Isaiah and Wyatt, then he hadn't slept at all. He was probably more exhausted than she was.

He adjusted the bag on his shoulder. "I need a place to drop my stuff until Isaiah gets here and we work out the logistics of making sure you stay safe back on home turf. I fly back home tomorrow. Isaiah didn't want you flying alone at the moment." He held up a hand. "I know you can take care of yourself, but—"

"But don't overlook the value of having someone to watch your back." As the elevator door slipped open, she met his eyes for the first time, guilt settling with an uncomfortable weight in her stomach. He'd given up his time to fly with her to Atlanta. Had sacrificed sleep and safety to be a second set of eyes for her. Instead of being a grouch, she ought to be grateful. Dana waited for the elevator doors to close. "I'm sorry. You're right. There's value in someone having your back."

"You're welcome."

"I didn't say… Oh, never mind." Offering him a small smile, she punched the button for the seventeenth floor. "I'm headed to the office as soon as I drop my stuff. I'm going to assume Isaiah already cleared you to come along."

"There's also value in having a valid security clearance." He nudged her arm with his elbow. "I get to see the Batcave."

"They'll only let you in so far. It's still WitSec, after all. Back when we had our hush-hush secret off-site offices, it actually would have been a little easier to get you in."

"Yeah. I heard about that place getting burned when Amy was on the run."

Dana grimaced. That had been a horrible night. A breached laptop had led the bad guys who were chasing Amy right to them. She still missed being in a regular office building with only her team present, a smaller family dynamic. Since they'd moved to a regular district office, the job felt more like work. Her space wasn't hers anymore. Other agents often wandered into her lab, and she often had to stop people from toying with her tech. Some stuff was too easy to mess up.

They stepped out into the narrow hallway. Although it was well lit, the windowless space still gave her a bit of claustrophobia every time she walked to her apartment. Being in the wide-open mountains for the past few days intensified the feeling. She'd forgotten what natural spaces felt like.

They felt like freedom. "Someday, I'm going to buy a house. Lots of windows. Lots of land." Why had she said that? It wasn't something she talked about. In her line of work, it was practically an impossible dream. The higher she climbed, the less attainable it became.

"Really?" Rich had fallen in behind her, likely because the hallway was too narrow for his broad shoulders to walk beside her. "I don't blame you. This is… All of the buildings around you, having to park in a parking deck, walk down this tiny hallway? Give me the sun and some space, please. I'm going to take a stab in the dark and say there are days you go from one parking deck to another without ever seeing the sky at all."

Hmm. Dana scanned the ceiling and pictured her

life. He was right. "Some days are like that." Okay, most days were like that. There were two balconies on her apartment. She hardly ever stepped foot onto them. It was so early when she went to work and so late when she got home. Even if she did venture out, the nearby buildings would probably cast her into shadow anyway.

"When I was a kid in upstate New York, I don't really remember ever being inside." Most of her memories involved exploring the woods in the summer and building snowmen in the winter. "I forgot how much I enjoyed being outside until this week. Hiking and cooking out was kind of fun."

"I can see you as the outdoorsy type."

A week ago, she'd have denied it, but after reconnecting with her nature-loving side, there wasn't an argument to give him. In fact, she sometimes dreamed of warm summer days outside with her parents.

Those dreams were better than the bloody nightmare she'd never been able to shake. Her mother once told her it came from a movie her father had let her watch when she was small, one too violent for her four-year-old mind to handle. She shuddered and pulled her keys from her pocket. "Doesn't matter. A country house is a big dream. The work I do for WitSec means I'll always live in the city and I'll always keep crazy hours. I'm needed at the bigger hubs. As I move up, the hubs will keep growing."

"Onward to DC?"

"Something like that." She glanced over her shoulder to flash a tight smile. "Because I'm never retiring." If she left the service, what would she do? Who would she be?

"I once thought the same about the army." The words were a mutter she probably wasn't meant to hear.

Yet he'd separated from the military. Had moved on to a career in law enforcement. Had formed a dream bigger than himself.

Dana slid the key in the lock and pushed the door open, then wheeled her suitcase into her apartment's small entryway. What would it be like to have a dream beyond today? One that focused more on others and less on herself? Did she even want one? To be honest, she wouldn't know where—

A rustle. Swift movement from the kitchen. A shadow flew, caught her shoulder and slammed her into the wall.

The sudden ferocity of the attack rooted Rich to the floor.

But only for a second.

A dark-haired man straightened to stand over Dana, who lay dazed in the narrow hallway. A knife glinted in his hand. "*Hola*, Danna." The man growled a variant of her name, more like *Donna* than *Dana*. He hadn't even noticed Rich.

However, Rich was about to make sure the guy was *very* aware of his presence. One step brought him close enough to grab the assailant's dominant wrist, then twist his hand and his weapon down away from him.

The knife clattered to the floor by Dana's head.

With a roar of rage and pain, the stranger tried to whirl on Rich.

But he countered the move, further twisting the man's arm up and behind his back. For a breath, he went limp. Rich shifted to drive him to the floor, but the narrow hallway made movement tricky. In the instant Rich was slightly off balance, the man turned and rotated away, sweeping Rich's foot from under him.

It wasn't a big move, but it was enough to loosen Rich's hold. Before he could regain his footing and his grip, the man grabbed his knife, slipped past and raced up the hallway.

Rich jumped up to follow suit but stopped, glancing from Dana to the doorway, where footsteps faded and a heavy door slammed. He couldn't leave her. There might be others waiting to attack.

Instead, he slammed the door with his foot and knelt beside her, sliding one arm around her shoulders to help her sit upright.

She winced when his hand brushed her right shoulder, but then she pulled away and scrambled to her feet. "How?" She tried to edge around him to the door. "How did he get in here? Why are you letting him get away?"

"Because you're my first priority."

"I'm fine."

Of course she was.

Rich wasn't going to argue with the red mark on her face that was already beginning to bruise or with the way she favored her shoulder where she'd crashed into the wall. Instead, he pulled two metal boxes from his duffel and passed one to Dana. He unlocked the other and removed his sidearm, then slipped the magazine into place. "Stay here. There may be more."

Dana opened her mouth to protest. He laid his finger against her lips.

Her eyes widened, and he took the opportunity to

speak before she could. "Unpack your weapon but stay put. Call the police."

He had to trust she'd obey.

The apartment wasn't very large. He peeked into the kitchen and the laundry room. Empty. Footfalls silent, he crept up the hallway and checked the small living room, where a wall of windows overlooked the skyline. Nothing moved.

The rest of the apartment was clear, as well. Nothing had been touched. It would be easy to tell if the place had been ransacked. It was sterile, no personal items cluttering the flat surfaces. No pictures on the walls. It was as if no one lived here. Dana had said she was married to her job, and her apartment seemed to agree.

She was standing in the living room when he returned. Although she appeared to be a bit pale and her hand shook as she brushed the hair out of her face, she stood her ground. Other than the minor injuries he'd noticed earlier, she appeared to be unharmed.

But appearances could be deceiving. "Did he hurt you?"

"Not bad enough to stop me. Cracked my shoulder into the wall, and I caught my cheek pretty good on the floor. Nothing to worry about."

Rich would beg to differ. He watched her as he retrieved his holster from his bag. "Shook you up, though."

She gave him a hard look. "You, too. You were a little slow on the uptake."

"Oh. Excuse me for being as caught off-guard as you were about the assailant hiding in your kitchen." If she was going to be flippant, so would he. Following her lead might net him more answers than arguing with her. "Did you recognize the guy?"

She hesitated, her hand hovering above the back of her sofa. She glanced away, then at him. "No."

He wasn't buying it. Her demeanor said differently. The shaking hand, the shifting motion of her eyes… no. Something more than being pitched into the wall was rattling her. "Talk to me, Dana."

She drew her finger along the back of the couch, acting as though she was going to ignore the request, but then her gaze caught his. "Nobody expects to get attacked in their own apartment." She shook her head and sank onto the arm of the sofa, her shoulders slumped in what he'd have called defeat on anyone else.

It almost made him want to cross the room and pull her into his arms, to protect her even more than he already had.

The thought shook him. He hadn't felt those kind of instincts since…

He inhaled sharply. Since Amber died in his arms. A shudder ran through him, and he shook the thought away. No. This was a favor to his friend Sam's teammate. Nothing personal. Nothing in it for him whatsoever. He was here to serve, to protect, to provide peace of mind to the people who worked with Dana and treated her as family. Nothing more.

Hopefully, she hadn't seen the emotion rocket through him.

He lifted his eyes to see if she had, but she was staring at her hands. Her expression was haunted, lost, almost as though she had left the room while her body stayed behind.

"Dana?"

"Do you ever…" She shook her head without looking up from her fingers. "Have you ever had a recurring nightmare?"

"Sure." The problems with his were they were grounded in a reality that assailed him when his guard was down in sleep. Those twisted visions were the reason he'd learned to subsist on only a few hours of downtime a night.

"Has part of your nightmare ever come true?"

Rich arched an eyebrow. While his were replays of events overseas soundtracked by Fitz's tortured cries and laced with the smell of gunfire and blood, he could honestly say he'd never had one repeat itself after the fact. "What do you mean?"

Her brow furrowed so deeply that a V drew between her eyes. Around her lips, a white line formed, almost as though she was trying to hold in some emotion she'd rather not let him see.

He couldn't do this anymore. Couldn't watch her hurt without offering her something. With a groan of surrender, he closed the space between them and pulled her to his chest in a hug he hoped brought comfort. His arms were so out of practice.

He'd expected her to fight. Instead, Dana pressed the backs of her hands against his chest and buried her face in her palms. She started to shake. Not with tears, but with something that might almost be fear.

Rich said nothing. Instead, he let her huddle against him and work out whatever terror and uncertainty the past twenty-four hours had wrought. Sooner or later, even a person as strong as Dana had to break down.

It was dangerous to keep it all inside. Eventually, it burst out and swamped you.

He should know.

Dana felt small and fragile in his arms, much like the way he'd known she would last night wearing his shirt and Amber's jeans.

He knew better than to believe the illusion. This woman had a spine made of steel. She wouldn't break. She'd pull herself up. Until she couldn't anymore.

He'd been there and done that. Trying to do it all alone had led him down a dark path swimming in alcohol and suicidal thoughts. It was a route he never intended to travel again. He wouldn't let Dana do the same, no matter how much she thought she could handle on her own. One day, the stress could wreck her.

When she spoke, he had to strain to hear the words muffled into her hands. "All my life I've had this awful dream. Sometimes it will go away for a year or so, then it comes back over and over for a while. Bad enough to make me not want to sleep."

Rich nodded. "I know." The words almost choked him. He'd seen the same bloody vision on repeat. Oddly, it was never Amber's death. It was always the horrific attack overseas that ended Fitz's life and left his team shattered. Sometimes he could even smell it during the day.

"I keep seeing this man and this woman. In the beginning of the dream, it's all safe and warm and… Maybe that's what makes the rest so awful." Dana shuddered and drew away from him. She walked to the window and stared at the city seventeen floors below, her finger running along the edge of the curtain. "It's like I'm watching from a distance. People talking. Arguing. Two men… They drag in this other man. He's…bruised. Bloody. Like he's been beaten. He's begging. A woman points at him, says something to the man she was arguing with, and he…"

She swallowed so hard, Rich could hear it from across the room. "He pulls out a gun and holds it to the begging man's head and pulls the trigger." Another shudder and she covered her face with her hands, almost as though she was trying to block out the image. "It's awful. But the worst part is he looks up at me after, like he's surprised, then angry. He shouts *Danna* at me. Then I wake up. Every time." She shook her shoulders and her hands as though trying to fling the vision away, then turned to finally meet his eye. "The man who was hiding in my house… He called me *Danna*."

Rich inhaled sharply. He'd heard it, too. He took a step closer to her then stopped when she held up her hands.

"How did he know to call me by a name I've only heard in nightmares?"

SIX

Dana slid her palms down her jeans and wanted to literally bite her tongue. Why had she spoken? Out loud, it sounded ridiculous, like a horror movie. Maybe he'd simply slurred her name. Maybe the shock had blasted her hearing. To think a stranger would call her by a name she'd never spoken aloud…

The way Rich looked at her, it was possible he thought the same thing, that she'd hopped off the reality train one station too early. His expression was too much like pity.

Or was it understanding?

Probably he thought the stress had broken her. Who babbled their nightmare had come true? She cleared her throat. "Then again, maybe I misheard him and he said my name like the other guy. Maybe I didn't hear right over the crash of my shoulder into the wall." But deep inside, no matter how much she argued with herself, Dana knew what she'd heard.

"No. You're right." Rich's voice was a low, deep rumble that brought the the same warmth she'd felt in his arms. A warmth she neither wanted nor needed. "I heard it. It sounded like Donna, only a little different."

The truth slid like ice down her spine. The name from her nightmare, only in a harsh whisper instead of a shout. Reality flipped onto itself. Maybe she was asleep and this was all a dream. Except she'd never had a nightmare as real as this one.

She didn't want to think about it anymore. Scrubbing her hands up and down her biceps, she headed for her suitcase, where it still lay in the hallway. "I need to go to work." To stay busy. To focus on people who needed her help to keep them safe.

"Shouldn't you wait for the police?"

She brushed past him. "I didn't call them."

His hand was a flash, his fingers loosely holding her arm before she could clear her way past him. "You didn't call? Why not? There was a man in your apartment, and he clearly wasn't here for coffee."

She'd been ready for his argument. "What are they going to do?" With a flick of her wrist, she freed herself from his hold. "We've already established this is targeted, so it's highly doubtful anyone else is in danger. When I get to work, I'll let my superiors know, and they can assign somebody to work it from there. I'm sure Isaiah will be on it the minute he lands, as well." She marched to the entry and grabbed the handle of her suitcase, then picked up the metal case that held her pistol. "He had on gloves, so there's no reason to dust for prints. It doesn't look like he touched anything, anyway."

A pounding at the front door had her reaching for the pistol that wasn't there.

In an instant, Rich had drawn his weapon and stood between Dana and the door.

Ire tamped down any remaining vestiges of fear.

Why did he insist on acting as though she couldn't take care of herself?

"Dana, it's Isaiah." His voice came with another trio of heavy-handed knocks. "Let us in."

Her brow furrowed and she glanced at Rich and mouthed, *"Us?"*

He shrugged. Clearly, he was as clueless as she was. If Sam had postponed his honeymoon to babysit her, she had a few choice words for him.

A quick peek through the peephole revealed Isaiah, along with his immediate supervisor, Deputy Marshal Brian Peterson. Her skin chilled. Things were a whole lot worse than she'd thought if Peterson had left his office to get involved. He was the kind of guy who could handle himself in the field but who enjoyed paperwork more. While he was incredibly straitlaced and by-the-book, he had gained the respect of the men and women who worked under him because he was fair and honest.

With a bracing breath, Dana pulled open the door and ushered the two men inside. "Come on in." There was no telling what bad news was headed her way now.

As he passed, Isaiah shot her a look she couldn't read, while Peterson refused to meet her eye.

The chill grew colder. Dana fought the urge to chew her bottom lip the way she used to as a child. "Isaiah, I though your flight was later."

"I caught an earlier one." He said something quietly to Rich, who stepped into the hall and closed the door.

Dana looked from the closed door to Isaiah, trying to communicate her silent questions with her expression. Why was Rich banished?

Isaiah didn't offer an explanation. He waved a hand as if he were ushering her into her own living room.

"You're going to want to sit down," he muttered as she passed. His hand rested on her shoulder briefly, then he pulled it away as though he didn't want to be caught supporting her.

Deputy Marshal Peterson stood by the patio door and tapped a manila folder against his thigh, watching the city outside the window. She might respect both of these men, but something inside her resented this intrusion into her personal space. This *second* intrusion into her personal space. Everything felt tilted, off balance. So little made sense.

Dana walked into her living room, but she refused to sit. "Deputy, I was on my way in to the office. May I ask what this is about?" Probably the attacks, but she didn't want to feed anyone a line.

"You tell me." He didn't turn, and his voice echoed slightly off the sliding glass door to the balcony. He was probably watching her reflection. Where he was usually friendly, he now sounded detached and emotionless.

Dana flicked a glance at Isaiah, who stood awkwardly in the middle of the living room between them, almost as though he could block whatever was coming. He stared at the wall with a tight-lipped glare. For a second, he caught her eye with a warning, then glanced at the back of the sofa before he looked away again.

Games had never been something Dana enjoyed. Not in her personal life and certainly not on the job. "With all due respect, sir, you came here. Whatever you're fishing for, there's nothing in the water to catch."

"I really hope that's true." Peterson turned suddenly, eyeing Dana as though he hated what he was about to do. "What's your name?"

"I'm sorry. *What?*" Had the man bounced his marbles down Peachtree Street? They'd worked together for five years. She glanced at Isaiah, then back at Peterson. "You know my name."

"Humor me."

The tension in the room drew so tight Dana could feel it press on her chest, stealing her breath. What was going on here? She'd been attacked three times. Now her supervisor wanted to play ridiculous games? The past twenty-four hours landed on her with a physical weight, rocking her back slightly. She took one step away and steadied her hand on the couch. Nothing made sense.

The motion pulled a deep frown from Isaiah, and it seemed to make Peterson even more grim than he had been before, almost as though he'd seen something he wished he hadn't. "Your name?"

Dana pulled herself to her full height. Whatever was happening, it had nothing to do with the attacks. "Dana Santiago."

"Not Danna Marquez?"

Only training kept her from gasping. *Danna.* The name the man had uttered in almost this same spot not even an hour ago. The same name from her nightmares. She waited for her breathing to regulate and forced out the words in a hard declaration. "My name is Dana Santiago."

"And your parents?"

"My father was Ramon Santiago. He died when I was a teenager. My mother is Karen Santiago." She turned to Isaiah, who continued to stare at the wall. "You've met her."

"Where were you born?"

Enough was enough. If he wanted to know these things, he could look in her file. She wasn't responding to any more questions, not when a would-be killer and her boss both uttered the same name in her presence. "Unless you give me a reason for this line of questioning, I'm not answering any more." She knew her rights, and she'd stand up for them. "I'd like to know where you came up with the name Danna Marquez. I'd also like to know why you're questioning my parentage and place of birth as though you don't already know. If I'm being accused of something, I have the right—"

"Your birthplace. Please."

"No." She looked at Isaiah for support, but he didn't offer any.

It was hard to tell if her team leader looked proud or worried. Possibly a little of both. He cleared his throat. "Where, Dana? The real where?"

The real where? He knew this. He'd met her mother on more than one occasion and had heard stories about her embarrassing exploits as a child. What in the world did he mean by that?

His chin lifted, and he turned to face her, his back fully to Deputy Marshal Peterson. "Answer the question." The words were firm, but his eyes pleaded. Something bigger than her birthplace was at stake here.

Her resistance ebbed. "Oswego, New York. I'm thirty-one years old. Born on October 17." Peterson could do the math to figure out the year.

Or he could read her file.

His expression unreadable, Deputy Peterson walked away from the window and settled into Dana's favorite chair, eyeing her. "This is the story you're sticking with?"

"Story?" Was he calling her a liar? "This is who I am. There's no story."

"The Marshals Service has placed you on administrative leave."

This time when Dana grabbed for the back of the couch, it was to prevent her weak knees from dumping her onto the floor. "What?" She whipped toward Isaiah. "Why am I on leave? What's the charge?" She'd been a rule follower her whole life. From the moment she'd taken the oath as a marshal, she'd executed her job with perfection.

"No charge. Yet." Peterson leaned forward in the chair, resting his hands on his knees. For the first time, his game face slipped, and he appeared sympathetic. "You may want to sit down, Dana. You're whiter than the walls in this place. How have you lived here this long and not decorated?"

The room actually spun from the whiplash conversation. She'd sit, but only because she might pitch onto her face if she didn't. "What is happening?" she asked, perching on the edge of the sofa.

Isaiah sat on the coffee table in front of her and forced her to look him in the eye. "There's suspicion you lied on your background checks and in your interviews for your security clearance."

Her head swiveled back and forth between the men, her brow furrowed. "They think I *lied*? About what?"

"Everything." Isaiah's voice rumbled low, angry. Not at her. At least, she *hoped* not at her. She silently begged him for answers he didn't offer. "Why would I lie?"

"Jairo and Rachel Marquez."

Dana jerked her head back, then shook it, confusion clouding her thoughts. "What do Argentinean arms dealers have to do with me?" The couple, who were well-known throughout every law enforcement agency in the country for funneling arms to the highest bidder, had a reputation for being ruthless. Suspicions ran high that at least two dozen murders on three continents could be pinned on the Marquez family.

No one in law enforcement had ever seen them. At least, no one had ever photographed them and lived to pass the pictures on.

"DEA finally got a man inside their organization." Peterson spoke for the first time in what seemed like hours. "He managed to get DNA and a passable picture of Rachel, though he's not been able to obtain one of Jairo yet." He passed the file to Isaiah.

"Okay…" But how did any of this make her a liar?

Isaiah stared at the file in his hand. "They did a routine database search, looking for close relatives who might be in the system. You know how it goes. If you can find a family member, you might be able to flip them and find a way in." He tapped the file against his palm then passed it to her. "They hit a familial match, a child."

"Somebody I know?" If she'd known she was friends with the child of notorious criminals, she'd have listed it on her clearance paperwork. A random association wouldn't be enough to suspend her, though.

She flipped the file open to find a photograph on top. A woman stood a distance from the camera, wearing slim jeans and a flowing green shirt. Long brown hair waved to her shoulders. She was elegant. Beautiful. And her face—

Dana gasped at the blow to her chest, at the flash of the woman from her nightmare, the woman who'd urged the murder of a begging victim. "Who is—?" The words hissed out on a roll of nausea. She swallowed and lifted her eyes to Isaiah's. "Who is this woman?"

He rested his hand on hers as if he could support her. "Rachel Marquez. DNA says she's your mother."

SEVEN

City lights stretched into the distance, blurring the late-night sky into black nothingness, too bright for the stars to shine. Christmas trees glimmered in apartment windows, and festive lights lined parks and streets. From below, the muffled sounds of traffic and music floated up in an indistinguishable chorus.

Dana slid deeper into the Adirondack chair her mother had given to her when she moved into the apartment. She pulled her knees against her chest, wrapped her arms around her legs, and held on tight.

Her *mother*.

Karen Santiago was shorter than Dana, heavier. A secretary for a trucking company in Oswego, she wore her jet-black hair in a chin-length bob and had an affinity for spaghetti and meatballs. Dana allowed a small smile. It always shocked everyone that the Argentinean lady would rather eat Italian food than her native fare.

The smile faded in a slight whimper. She would not cry.

Her native country. Argentina. Where elegant, murderous Rachel Marquez and her husband, Jairo, held large-caliber pistols to men's skulls and pulled the trigger.

Dana jerked, winced. The DNA results had to be wrong.

But if they were, how had she conjured the image of a coldhearted killer into her nightmares? How had she heard a name no one should know? How could she have the same eyes, nose and chin as the killer in that photograph?

Behind her, the glass door slid along its track, bringing with it the smell of coffee and the presence of a man she was almost glad had stuck around when everyone else had left.

Rich appeared at her right, holding out a mug. "It's black. The way you like it."

Tilting her head to look up at him, Dana reached for it. The ceramic warmed her palms. She was cold from the inside out, but this helped a little. Likely it was more the gesture than the beverage. "Is coffee your answer to everything?"

Rich settled on the concrete floor with his back against the railing. He bent his legs, rested his elbows on his blue-jeaned knees, then screwed up his lip in a way that was probably meant to be comical. "Tired? Coffee. Sluggish? Coffee. Sad? Coffee works for everything else. Why not try?" He took a sip from the mug cradled in his hands and met her eye over the rim. "How're you doing?"

"I don't know." It was an honest answer. She bounced from numb to angry to shocked back to numb in a nauseating cycle that made her insides quiver. Probably caffeine wasn't the answer, but it seemed nothing was. Not even prayer. The words wouldn't form. "The DNA has to be wrong."

Rich took another sip and waited for her to choose reality over denial.

He didn't have to speak. Dana knew the truth. She was a high-percentage match to both Jairo and Rachel. Too high for coincidence.

"Have you talked to your mom yet?"

"Which one? The liar or the murderer?" The words snapped brittle in the winter air. No, she hadn't called Karen Santiago. This was a conversation best had in person, where Dana could watch see her reactions. Where there wouldn't be time for her to calculate another lie.

Her bitterness was an emotion Rich didn't deserve. He could be cozied up at his mountain cabin right now, with football on the TV and Christmas lights on the tree, but he was here with her.

This mess wasn't his fault. If anything, he was doing his best to stand as a buffer between Dana and a nightmare she couldn't leave behind. "I'm sorry. I…" She waved a hand as though she could swipe the words away before they reached his ears. "This hasn't been my best day."

"Can't say I blame you." He set the coffee mug beside him and rested his hands on his thighs. "Pretty sure your life was put into a blender last night and someone kicked it up to high."

His understanding pricked something behind her eyes, but she swallowed the accompanying lump in her throat. Nope. No matter what life threw at her, she *wasn't* going to cry. She wasn't that kind of girl. "What else could possibly happen?"

Rich stopped moving and tilted his head to look at her, one eyebrow raised. "In my experience, you don't ask if you don't want to find out the answer."

He could say that all he wanted, but as far as she was concerned, it really couldn't get much worse. In the space from one sunset to another, she'd lost everything.

She couldn't even talk to God.

Thoughts and words jumbled into a nameless emotion that pressed her from the inside out. Without release, she'd explode. "When I woke up this morning, there was no question who I was, you know? I mean, twenty-four hours ago I was beside you and fighting for my life, but I was still… I was still *me*." Digging her fingers into the coffee mug, she stared across the city lights, envying every window where Christmas lights twinkled and people prepared for their holidays with friends and family. All of them were content with their identities, knowing what they were going to do tomorrow and the next day… "If I'm not Deputy Marshal Dana Santiago, born in Oswego to Ramon and Karen Santiago, and a tech-geek rock star, then—"

The words cracked, fell to the floor and shattered along with her emotions. The tears wouldn't be swallowed, wouldn't be beaten into submission. They flowed freely down her face.

She couldn't even be the strong woman who never cried. Even that was gone. *If I'm not me, then who am I?*

Dana leaned forward and pressed her leaking eyes against her knees, vaguely aware she might shatter the coffee mug in her ever-tightening grip. She would not sob. She would not break, not alone and certainly not in front of this man who probably thought she was weak after rescuing her three different times.

The only sound was her ragged breathing until a soft shuffle came from the right. If Rich was smart, he'd go inside, shut the door and leave the disintegrating woman on the porch to blow away like dust in the wind.

"Hey." The word was a soft whisper, a gentle tug back to reality. "Dana, hey." Gentle hands wrapped around her ankles and eased her feet to the floor.

Dana wanted to curl into a ball and shield herself from his concern and understanding, but her muscles wouldn't let her. Over the years, she'd comforted witnesses and their families, but when was the last time someone had made her a priority? While her mind wanted her to stay fearless and strong, her heart wanted another human being to understand.

She kept her eyes closed. Pity would undo her once and for all.

Rich eased the cup from her fingers, then tapped her forehead. "Look at me."

It took a second, but she finally convinced herself to peel her eyes open.

Rich knelt in front of her, hands resting on the arms of her chair. When she made eye contact, he offered a ghost of a smile, almost triumphant but not gloating. No, it was more like he was glad she'd actually responded. "You are still Dana Santiago, tech-geek rock star." He punctuated the last four words by tapping his index finger against her knee. "Nobody can take that away from you."

But they had. How was she going to prove she hadn't known all along? That she hadn't lied her way into this position? Above all, the government officials who handed out security clearances hated a liar. It was the quickest way to ensure being blackballed at the federal level. How could she convince them the lies were *to* her, not *from* her?

Watching the dawn raise light over a city was nothing like watching the sun lift itself over the mountains, that was for sure. But while Rich's heart longed to be home, his head agreed with Isaiah and Wyatt that he needed to be with Dana.

Right now, he was all she had.

He shoved his phone into his hip pocket. His conversation with Isaiah had honestly gotten them nowhere. While everyone else's focus had shifted to Dana's parentage and the threat to her job, Rich's stayed lasered on the most pressing matter. Someone was trying to kill Dana, and she needed to go into hiding. The threat might or might not be connected to her blood family. No one seemed to know.

A large problem loomed over the entire situation. Until her name was cleared and she was reinstated, there was nothing Isaiah or the other members of her team could do to help. They had another agency investigating the attacks, but she was cut off from her team and their vast network of secure locations. As long as she was suspended, she couldn't communicate with them. Worse, because she wasn't a witness in need of protection, they couldn't even offer her shelter.

Rich stretched his feet until they bumped the balcony railing and tried to ease some of the stiffness out of his joints. He'd spent the night sitting in an armchair, facing the door to her apartment, and had only stepped out on the balcony this morning to make phone calls to Wyatt and Isaiah. While Dana couldn't have contact with her team, no rule said Rich couldn't.

It would be nice if he could say it had been a long time since he pulled an all-nighter on guard duty. But it had only been about a year and some change since he'd helped Sam hide Amy.

Only they'd failed. Rich had been the one patrolling the perimeter when the bad guys struck. Amy had nearly died.

His fault. Just like his fiancée.

Well, this time was different. This time he wasn't going to leave someone who was targeted out in the open, arrogantly thinking he could keep them safe from any threat. He'd find Dana a place to hide. Oh, he'd stay close, but he wasn't having her run around in the open while there was a target between her shoulders.

The shoulders that had quaked in his arms.

What had he been thinking? He hadn't held a woman since Amber died.

Until Dana's utter despair floored him. He didn't have the right to hold her, but he'd had to do something. The need to shield and protect had felt right in a way that hadn't felt right since Amber died.

That terrified him more than armed assassins.

He scratched his cheek and itched two days' worth of stubble. It reminded him of being outside the wire overseas, hunting down bad guys.

Felt kind of like now. Dana couldn't stay in her apartment. Someone knew where she lived. Even though they were seventeen stories up and the crew after Dana had more of an affinity for knives than rifles, the balconies and the floor-to-ceiling windows made him more than a little uneasy. He had to get her out of here. Soon.

Isaiah had agreed.

Soft sounds floated through the open glass door. Dana was up, although if she was anything like him, she hadn't slept at all.

Rich shoved out of the chair and walked into the apartment to find her wearing track pants and a sweatshirt, staring into the refrigerator. It was doubtful she saw what was in front of her.

She looked up when he walked in. "I was thinking eggs, but now I'm not." She slammed the door and leaned against the fridge. "You flying home today?"

Only if she was going with him. "We'll see." He held up a hand to stop her as she straightened to argue. "Neither of us is staying here, though. They've come at you in your apartment once. You aren't sitting around here and waiting for them to ambush you again."

"Hadn't planned to." She crossed her arms over her chest, defiant to the core. "I'm going to Oswego."

She was…*what*? The woman made him understand why his mom had often pinched the bridge of her nose when he'd declared his intentions to do something completely idiotic as a kid. "Oswego?"

"I want to talk to my…to the woman who raised me. To my mother." She swallowed the word, mumbling it instead of giving it the force it deserved. "I want to see her face-to-face. I need answers, and she's the only one who has them."

"Have you lost every one of your senses?" His voice kicked up, driven by hot fear that ran all over him at the thought of her not only out in the open, but far away from protection, too. "That's the most dangerous thing you can do. You may be cut off from WitSec, but I can still get you somewhere safe and out of the way."

"How long should I run?" Dana banged a fist on the refrigerator door behind her and straightened, squaring off as though she was ready for war. "A week? A year? A decade? What if we never find out who's behind this? Do you want me to hide forever? What am I supposed to do? Knit? Collect stamps? Or, better yet…" She pulled herself even taller. "I can build a cabin in the woods and isolate myself from everybody. Won't you teach me all you know, oh wise one?"

Wow. The venom in her words burned his skin, but he didn't back down. Too much was at stake. "It's safer if you're not in the open."

"You think I don't know? You know who I work for, right? I've said the same thing a thousand times to dozens of scared witnesses. I know it's true, but I also know there's no way to clear my name if I'm locked away in some remote location or in some soulless corporate apartment in the middle of some random city."

"Like this one?" He didn't even know why he'd said it. It was ugly, but he was scared for her.

Dana flinched, then glanced around the apartment. Her shoulders visibly sagged, almost as though his comment had dragged her back into reality. "At your place, I actually wondered if you'd let me pay you to decorate mine." She shook her head and stared at something behind him in the living room. "I hear everything you're saying. Common sense and every ounce of my training says hiding is the best choice. I've preached that to witnesses for years." She sighed, and the lines on her forehead deepened. "But it's not who I am."

The words were soft, but they slammed into his chest, the vocal reminder of her fear the night before, of her pain. Of his inability to fix any of this.

"Rich, I may not know a lot of things, including my own name, but I do know not seeking answers will kill me."

It was his turn to flinch. Allowing Amber to remain in the open had killed her, but Dana wasn't Amber. She was trained for this. As much as it chilled him from the inside out, she was right. Dana was like a shark. If she wasn't moving, wasn't working to figure this out, she might survive physically, but the emotional and mental toll could take her to a place from which she might never return.

"I need answers."

"Well, you aren't going alone." She needed eyes behind her as well as in front of her. If she thought he was going to let her waltz down to her car and take off on a twenty-hour drive by herself, she had better think again.

"You have a job to do, Rich. A life in Mountain Springs. I'm sure Wyatt needs you back on patrol. The department—"

"Wyatt's the one who sent me here with you. *You're* my job."

"Your job." The words were flat, her forehead tight. "I'm outside the Mountain Springs PD's jurisdiction, aren't I?" She shoved away from the fridge and walked to the cabinet, pulling it open with a jerk that should have torn the door off the hinges. Her back was to him, her shoulders a tense line. "Tell him you need a new assignment. This one's over."

"No."

Those straight shoulders grew tighter. "No?"

"No." He was messing this up in two hundred ways. Digging his fingernails into his palms, Rich walked to the bar that separated the small kitchen from the rest of the apartment and rested his fists on the cool granite. "It's not just the job. I mean, technically, it can't really be my job, but... We share the same friends. That makes us... I don't know."

"Distant relatives?" Her voice inched up a notch, maybe with a bit of amusement.

At least she heard what he was trying to say. "In a weird sort of way." Before, he'd felt a sense of duty in watching over her, but now that they'd broken down a barrier and he'd held her, he felt a different sort of protectiveness kick in. This was more than keeping someone safe. It had somehow turned into keeping someone he cared about safe.

Keeping *a friend* out of harm's way.

A friend.

Nothing more.

He rapped his knuckles on the counter. "I'm guessing you have a grand plan to make your way to Oswego without being intercepted by your entourage?"

Dana pulled a box of cereal and two bowls from the cabinet, stopped at the fridge for a carton of milk, then slid a bowl and spoon to him. She opened the box then handed it to him. "Let's just say I have friends in high places." She held her hand flat and swooped it through the air.

"A pilot?" Guess she'd accepted his presence, since

she was sharing her plans. Or she'd decided to drug him and sneak off while he was lights out.

She nodded and took the cereal box after he finished pouring his. "She has a small jet and a need for some flight hours. If you insist on going, then she'll fly both of us into Watertown, where she's visiting family. We can rent a car from there. It's about an hour's drive. The big issue will be getting from here to the airport."

Actually, that might be the easy part. He'd plotted several ways to get her out of the building during his long night on guard duty. Rich pulled his phone from his pocket and dialed. "I'll handle that. Just let me know what time you want to leave."

Dana swallowed a bite of cereal and arched an eyebrow. "Who are you calling?"

"The cavalry."

EIGHT

Light snow dusted the ground beside the two-lane country road, illuminated by the headlights of the SUV they'd rented in Watertown. One thing Dana had never gotten used to about the South…it hardly ever snowed. In upstate New York, they practically skipped fall and jumped straight into winter. In Georgia there were years when summer never surrendered at all. It seemed to be even worse in the city, where an inch of snow could gridlock the greater Atlanta area for hours.

The city. Dana glanced in the rearview, found it was still clear, then took in the tall trees and the occasional field. Until she'd visited Mountain Springs, she'd forgotten how much she loved living in the country, where the air was clean and the stars were visible. In fact, she hadn't realized until she was in Mountain Springs that she couldn't remember the last time she'd taken a deep breath. Atlanta was amazing, but it had never felt like home.

Maybe that was why her apartment still looked as though no one lived there.

In the passenger seat, Rich stirred and crossed his arms over his chest. He'd fallen asleep not long after they hit the road to Oswego, and she'd left him alone. Knowing him, it had been almost two days since he'd let his guard down enough to sleep. Either he trusted her to drive them safely or he knew he'd reached his physical limit. Given that his control-freak self hadn't argued about driving in the first place, it was probably the latter. Even hard-core soldiers needed rest now and then.

Soldiers. With another check of the rearview, Dana allowed herself a grin, largely to cover up her churning stomach as the miles to her childhood home disappeared under the tires.

Rich had called in the cavalry, all right. A buddy of his in Columbus rode with a veterans' motorcycle association and was able to round up seven similar Harleys in a short time. Right after lunch, they'd roared up the street, the sound of their V-twin engines reaching all the way to the seventeenth floor. After some quick introductions, one couple stayed back in her apartment while Dana and Rich geared up in leathers and helmets. While no one was dressed exactly alike, it had been nearly impossible to tell who was who. The pack left the building and branched off one by one throughout Atlanta. If anyone was following, they were likely incredibly confused and unspeakably frustrated by the end of their ride.

It had been years since she'd been on the back of a bike, and for a brief moment when they headed south toward the small airport in Cusseta, she'd almost forgotten why the subterfuge had been necessary in the first place. Either she was going to have to learn to ride when this whole thing was over, or she'd have to find a friend who'd let her tag along.

Like Rich. Who apparently owned two motorcycles and was rebuilding a third.

He was a bigger surprise at every turn. Like the way he'd known to comfort her without getting too close.

She stole a quick peek at him as he dozed in the passenger seat, his face shadowed by the dim interior lights. In sleep, the stress and worry that seemed to dog his every step vanished. Other than the few days' worth of beard darkening his cheeks and jaw, he looked like he must have looked as a young boy.

"You ought to be watching where you're going." He shifted, straightened and opened his eyes.

Yes. Yes, she should. Dana turned her full attention back to the road.

"You shouldn't have let me sleep." He stretched his legs as much as he could and reached his hands behind him in a full-on cat pose. "Somebody needs to be watching the mirrors."

"Unless they're driving without lights, which would be incredibly dangerous out here, we don't have a tail. Even superheroes have to sleep sometime. You were about six seconds from a crash and burn."

He dismissed her with a *humph* and glanced at his watch. "We must be getting close."

They were.

The closer they got, the more Dana wanted to pull over the rented SUV and hide in the woods. Home had always been a safe place, but now…

Her hand resting on the gearshift gripped tighter. If her mother wasn't her mother and her name wasn't her name and her childhood home wasn't her home, then there was no telling who she really was. No telling what horrible things lived dormant inside her, waiting for the wrong moment to rise up.

It was possible there was no safe place for her anymore.

Rich reached over and laid his hand, warm and gentle in a way that didn't match him at all, on hers. "You know, we rented this truck with my credit card. I'd like to not have to pay damages for your permanent finger marks in the vinyl."

His unexpected touch ran warmth all the way up her arm and into her stomach. The quiver had nothing to do with the fear and trepidation she'd felt since they touched down in Watertown. This was a lot more pleasant.

And a lot more unsettling.

She withdrew her fingers and gripped the steering wheel with both hands. "We're less than ten minutes away."

"Then you'll have answers."

"To questions I don't want to ask. Questions I shouldn't *have* to ask."

Rich watched her for a second, kneading his knee with his left hand, then looked away.

"Your knee bothering you?"

"What? No." He snapped to attention, then stared out the window. "Sure are a lot of houses lit up for Christmas out here."

Dana let the change of subject take hold. He'd been wounded overseas, that much she knew, but she didn't know the extent or even the location. It didn't matter. Apparently, she was traveling with a real-life hero, according to some things Sam had said in the past.

Easier to think about this than what was coming

in the next ten minutes. "Christmas is different here. I mean, it's…slower. At least in my head it is." Memories of visits with other families, parties at church, gifts left on front porches. "My mom's best friend owns a Mexican restaurant not too far from here, on the outskirts of town. She always had a big bash one week before Christmas Eve with all sorts of gifts and Christmas karaoke and other stuff."

"That was last night." Rich's voice was low.

Dana scanned the road ahead as though it would show her a calendar. "Christmas Eve is less than a week away?" She hadn't bought anything. Hadn't considered whether or not she'd come home for Christmas. How had she missed it? Even before her life blew up, she'd forgotten Christmas?

How would this year play out? Everything was falling apart. Even her memories held a false tone. Instead of bringing warmth, they clanged a hollow ring. Part of her longed to walk through the front door as though this was a surprise holiday visit, to pretend all was well and her family was her family. To make cookies with her mother. To relive the innocence of Christmas Eve church services and Christmas morning gifts. To feel the warm fuzzies she'd lost long before tonight.

But she couldn't. There was too much at stake. Too much had changed.

The familiar entrance to the driveway made her stomach roil.

She turned in to the driveway, navigating the narrow path through the trees. When she was younger, her dad had complained about having to hook the snowplow to the front of his truck so he could get to the mailbox.

Her dad. Who actually wasn't her dad.

Dana chewed on the inside of her lower lip as the headlights swept the front of the two-story vinyl-sided house. It was dark, although it was not quite eight. Either her mom was at her friend Stephanie's restaurant or she'd already gone to bed.

Dana was about to wake her up.

She killed the engine and reached for the door, but Rich's hand on her shoulder stopped her. "What?"

"Front door's open."

Icy fear and hot anger blended in Dana's veins in a sickening soup. She drew her pistol. "I'll go in the front and clear the house. You don't know the layout. You take the back. Make sure no one heads out. Be careful. My mother is the one who taught me how to shoot." He'd cleared a house before, but her mother didn't know him. No sense in getting Rich killed by friendly fire. The thought made her blood even colder.

"If anyone's inside, they've seen the headlights, but kill the interior lights," he told her. "At least they won't be able to tell how many of us there are."

It took a second in the unfamiliar car, but she located the button and shut down the door lights.

Almost with the same motion, they eased out of the vehicle and crept toward the house.

Dana kept to the side and eased up the steps, out of the direct line of sight of the door. Outside, she stopped to listen and to give Rich time to get into position. She took two deep breaths and tried to shove her emotions aside, to make this simply a home entry and not a mission with serious personal stakes.

She'd count to five for Rich to be in place, then enter. *One.* Her grip on her pistol tightened.

Two. One foot slipped forward.

Three. Something shuffled behind her.

She pivoted on one heel, but a massive force slammed into her head, knocking her into the bushes beside the porch.

The cry from the front of the house set Rich into motion before the faint echo died away.

Dana.

He never should have left her alone. His gut had told him to follow her into the house, but he'd obeyed her order, heeded her plan. He'd followed a valid tactical plan instead of remembering Dana was in danger and he was here to keep her safe.

Whatever happened to her would be his fault.

At the corner of the house, he skidded to a stop on damp leaves and snow, nearly dropping to one knee. He forced himself to act out of his rational mind and not out of his wildly misfiring emotions. Running blind around the corner might get him killed.

He inhaled cold night air, counted to three and focused on the next step. Holding his sidearm low, he peeked around the house and tried to distinguish shadows. In the faint moonlight, a figure stood on the porch with its back to Rich and looked down into the bushes.

Rich eased around the corner. The figure was too big to be Dana. Definitely a male. Tall. Broad. Light reflected off an object in his right hand.

Another knife. There was definitely continuity in the choice of weapons, which indicated one group in play rather than a random hodgepodge of assassins.

It was better than a pistol. Creepier, but better, because Rich having a firearm definitely gave him the advantage.

As long as the guy didn't have a partner waiting in the woods.

The man shouted something in Spanish, but the words weren't familiar. He raised the knife.

Rich aimed and swallowed the unfamiliar mass in his throat that threatened to choke his words into use-lessness. "Drop the knife!" The shout echoed off the trees.

With a jerk, Dana's assailant turned. In the pale moonlight, his face was featureless, menacing beneath a dark mask.

"You heard me." Rich held his aim level at center mass and stepped slowly closer. The last thing he wanted to do was shoot a man, but the thought of Dana dead or injured made his trigger finger twitch. "Lay down the knife. Keep your hands where I can see them."

"You are the big hero again, *Espectro*?" The man shifted his grip on the knife, as though he prepared to throw it. "You will force us to kill you before we carry out our plans for Danna."

Espectro? And that name again, *Danna*. Rich forced his mind to center. "Lay down the knife. Keep your hands where I can see them."

"You will have to shoot me first." He raised the knife, his arm drawing up and back to throw.

A shadow shifted in the bushes behind the man, and a dark figure caught him in the back of the legs. He went down hard on his knees with a sickening thud. The knife clattered off the porch and into the bushes.

Rich ran forward as Dana stood at full height in the

bushes beside the porch, but the assailant rolled to the side and raced down the steps, heading for the trees at full speed, although a limp likely slowed him some.

Rich pursued, but he stopped at the wood line. It was too dark to see, and running into the trees without an idea of where he was going was foolish.

Besides, he wouldn't leave Dana alone again. Bad things happened when he went his own direction. When he left the women in his care to their own devices. Tonight had only reinforced that truth.

"Have you lost your mind?" Her footsteps pounded closer behind him. "Go after him!"

Rich turned on his heel and caught Dana around the waist as she tried to pass. He spun her toward him and pulled her to his chest with one arm. He holstered his pistol and wrapped his other arm around her. She was fighting too hard for him to keep her in place one-handed. "Dana, stop. Think about what you're doing."

The side of her fist landed against the scar on his shoulder, the spot still tender even though more than two years had passed. "You're letting him go."

"I'm saving your life." He tightened his arms around her back. "You're not thinking. You're acting on emotion. Remember your training, Dana."

"You're letting…" With a huff she stopped fighting and sagged, her forehead against his chest, her breathing heavy. She stayed there, her inhales gradually shifting from ragged to calm.

Rich kept his eyes on the trees and his ears on the night sounds, listening for their anonymous "friend's" return, but he heard nothing except Dana's breathing. His hold on her gradually shifted, from defensive to soothing, until he'd pulled her close in a way that surpassed the comfort he had offered her earlier.

This time he *wanted* to hold her close. He *wanted* to be near her. His eyes slipped closed. Since Amber's death, he hadn't wanted to hold another woman.

Until now.

With a ragged breath of his own, Rich set Dana away from him. Now it was *his* emotions running away with rational thought. A killer likely lurked nearby, and here he stood in the open with Dana, acting as though the only thing that mattered in the world was how she made him feel.

The exact same thing that had led to Amber's murder.

Rich was out of bounds. Getting attached was foolish when he couldn't plan a future. Letting her become a distraction was a danger to both of them. "We have to go. Now." Her attacker could return at any moment, and he likely would not come back alone.

"My mother." Dana backed farther away and turned toward the house. "She might be inside. He might have gotten to her first. She might be…"

There was no need to finish. Her worst nightmares might be true inside her childhood home.

Rich prayed not. It was one thing to lose a parent. But another entirely to lose one with so many questions unanswered. *Lord, let Dana's mother be safe. Let her be anywhere but here.*

Without looking at him, Dana headed toward the house. "My gun's in the bushes." She marched into the shrubs beside the porch, knelt down and came back with her weapon in hand. "His knife's there, too. We'll get it on the way out." She took the steps two at a time.

Rich caught her before she opened the front door. "Me first."

"My mother. My house."

"Your life." He dropped his voice to a whisper, laid a hand on her biceps and shifted her behind him. "You're too emotionally involved. You'll miss something." Holding out his hand, he waited for her to drop a key into it. She was bound to have one.

She muttered something under her breath but handed him her keys. "As soon as we get in the door, I'm turning on the lights. Nobody gets to hide from me here."

Not even her mother, Rich was sure. He was three steps into the house when the room illuminated. The glare forced him to blink a few times before his sight cleared.

He stood in the middle of a large living room. Below the front window, a couch stood sentinel, facing a TV mounted over a brick fireplace. A fully decorated Christmas tree filled one corner of the room, the limbs heavy with homemade decorations. The space was pristine. "I expected it to be tossed."

"Same." Dana's voice was grim, but it had lost that emotional edge. "I'll take upstairs. You take down. We'll meet in the kitchen."

"We go together." No way was he letting her out of his sight again.

"Have it your way." Methodically, they cleared the house. No hidden attackers. No sign of Dana's mother. The only indication she'd been here recently was her cell phone, lying on a table next to the back door, the battery dead.

In the kitchen, Dana holstered her pistol. "Her car's gone. She could be anywhere."

"Would she take off without her cell phone?"

With a shrug, she rounded the island and leaned back against the counter, staring at the back door. "It wouldn't be unusual. My mother was never a big fan. Took me years to get her to carry one at all. She doesn't trust technology—says the more you have, the more privacy you give away."

"She's not wrong."

"You have no idea how right she is. In my line of work…" She shoved away from the counter and pulled the fridge open.

In her line of work, she probably knew thirty-seven ways to hack his smartphone. "Any clues in the fridge?" It wouldn't have been his first place to look, but she knew what she was searching for. Either that, or she was hungry.

"She was here today. There's deli meat purchased this afternoon." Shutting the door, she eyed him up and down, her expression dark. Something more than her mother's whereabouts seemed to be bothering her.

"What?" She was thinking something, and Rich wasn't sure if he wanted to know what. Not with that look of concern on her face.

"The man outside. He called you *Espectro*. It means ghost."

"I heard. He also called you *Danna*. They definitely know who you really are."

"I'm more concerned they know who you are." She held a hand out to him, almost as though she wanted him to come closer, then let it drop. "If you have a name, an identifier with them, then you're on their radar."

She was probably right. The military worked with the same parameters. People in the spotlight had nicknames that often grew larger than their actual personas.

But his safety wasn't the issue here. "It doesn't matter right now. We need to get you out of here before he comes back with reinforcements. They want you dead, Dana. They won't miss a chance to come at you while they know where you are. It's time to go."

"My mother." She turned a slow circle and surveyed the kitchen. "There has to be a way to warn her, a way they wouldn't know."

"We'll call the cops from the road, report a break-in, then set up a meeting with her remotely. We'll call from my cell, since yours is still in Mountain Springs."

"I wish—wait." Dana stepped toward the refrigerator, staring at the photos there. "A way to warn her…"

Her face relaxed. A slight smile tugged at her mouth. Turning on her heel, she reached into a drawer, retrieved a zip-top bag and headed for the front door. "Let's get that knife and get out of here. I know where she is." She glanced over her shoulder at Rich. "She knew this was coming."

NINE

Christmas lights reflected on snow-dampened streets, playing with the contrast between illumination and shadows. It might be pretty, but all of the visual chaos was a tactical nightmare.

Rich shifted in the passenger seat, keeping a wary eye on the road before and behind them. As far as he could discern, they hadn't picked up a tail. His shoulder ached from the cold, but he refused to massage it. Dana had started to be cognizant of his small movements and had begun to ask too many questions. Telling the story of the day Fitz died while his entire team listened in helpless horror wasn't on his agenda tonight.

Or ever, really.

He tilted his neck slightly. Maybe that would help with the shoulder. It didn't. "So, we're going to your friend's restaurant after all?" Other than their destination, Dana had said little since they left her mother's house.

"Yes. But not my friend. She's my mother's best friend."

Funny how she always used the word *mother*. It

seemed formal for what he knew of her. Had she always used that name? Or had the past twenty-four hours subconsciously robbed Dana of her sense of family?

If he woke up tomorrow and found out his mom and dad weren't his blood family and his real parents were internationally wanted criminals, would it change him?

More red and green Christmas lights blurred past. With two brothers in the house, Christmases had always been loud and more than a little rambunctious. Seemed like something always got broken in the wrapping-paper madhouse. Yet, somehow, whenever his dad read the story of Jesus's birth on Christmas Eve, there was a blessed moment of silence. A certain feeling in those few minutes that found a way into his heart with a peace he hadn't felt in years. For an instant, he was ten years old without a care in the world other than trying to figure out how a great big God could fit into a tiny little baby. Even better, why a great big God would even want to do such a thing.

If he found himself swamped with the revelations Dana was processing, it would tear something inside him. Somehow, the memories would be tainted and false. It wasn't hard to imagine distancing himself with a more formal title for Mom.

Dana cleared her throat as she slowed at a flashing yellow light and turned left. "If she hasn't blown town completely, she's there. She knows she's in danger."

If that was the case, why hadn't she reached out to Dana to warn her? He could ask, but it was a rhetorical question that might only bring her more pain. "How did you figure that out?" There had been no note on the refrigerator, just family photos and random magnets.

"I was probably in middle school. It wasn't long after my father died, and I always chalked it up to the paranoia of a newly widowed single mother, but now…" She drew in a deep breath. "Now so much makes sense. My mother is a little rigid in how she likes things, so the pictures on the fridge always stayed in the same spots. She used to tell me if I ever came home from school and I saw them rearranged a certain way, then I should hide and wait for *Tía* Stephanie. When I was older, she told me to get in the car and go straight to the restaurant."

"They were different tonight."

"Death Valley on the top. An old-fashioned wanted poster we had taken at some ghost town in Arizona in the middle. Me holding a stuffed dog named Taco on the bottom."

Rich nodded, but he kept his mouth closed. Something deep-seated was happening in Dana's family. The average mother didn't create a covert messaging system for her child. He'd thought she was simply adopted somehow, but now things pointed to something much more dangerous.

Dana pulled the SUV behind a large cream-colored stucco building with an arch above the front door and shut off the engine.

Time to move. Rich shoved his phone into his pocket and peeked at the knife he'd stashed in the glove box. He'd texted photos of the weapon to Isaiah, who he could still legally contact, even if Dana couldn't due to her suspension. The intricate markings on the blade had to mean something. If those images rested in a database anywhere, Dana had assured him Isaiah knew people who could find them.

Rich started to close the glove box, but she laid her hand on his forearm. "Bring it with us."

He flinched at her touch. The whole ride he'd done everything he could to focus on the job at hand and not on how she'd felt in his arms on the front lawn. While they should have been focused on the attacks on her, on whether or not her mother was safe in the house, he'd been mooning like a teenage boy with a crush on the head cheerleader.

He'd lost his edge. Had reacted emotionally instead of responding tactically.

He could have gotten them both killed. It was clear he'd learned nothing.

Rich sighed. There was nothing he could do now but remain vigilant and not let it happen again. He retrieved the knife and shut the glove box. "Are you ready for this?"

She stared at the back door of the restaurant and said nothing.

Behind that door rested answers, held by a woman who'd hidden the truth from Dana for years. Even with good reason, that had to feel like a betrayal. "You've come this far. If you won't go into hiding, then you have to confront this now, before the bad guys figure out where you went and make another move against you." Time wasn't a commodity they could squander.

"You're right." Dana shoved open the door and marched toward the back of the restaurant, which was still hopping even though it was past the traditional dinner hour. Music was muffled outside the building. Sounded like someone singing off-key karaoke.

Rich hurried to catch up with her. A single street-light lit the back parking lot. Several garbage cans stood behind a fence at the rear, and a wooden garage sat farther back at the edge of the property. Too many shadows. Too much darkness.

Dana pounded on the large metal back door with her fist. "It's Dana. Open up." Stepping back, she looked up, straight into a camera mounted above their heads.

The door swung open. Someone pulled her inside.

Rich had to rush to make it around the door before it slammed shut and left him standing on the wrong side. He slipped in and lifted his head.

Only to find a pistol aimed at his chest.

Whoa. Gun.

Javier Figueroa leveled a pistol at Rich, likely unsure if he was the good guy or the bad guy. From her mother, Dana knew he'd been recently sworn in as a law enforcement officer and was in protective mode.

She eased between Rich and Javi. "You can lower the weapon, Javi."

"You're sure?" His dark eyes scanned her face for any signs of distress, but he slowly lowered the weapon.

"He's with me." Honestly, Rich was the reason she was safe, but that wasn't something to admit. At her mother's house, she'd practically melted in his arms, and it wasn't the first time. While he held her, she'd forgotten everything but him and the way she felt an odd, peaceful sense of safety she'd never felt before.

It only lasted a moment. The situation was humiliating and made her look like the rookie she hadn't been in years. Proving herself capable all over again was of no interest to her, but if she didn't stop acting like a damsel in distress, she'd find herself doing just that.

Javi holstered his pistol. "Your mom thought you were dead. She's here, but I'm guessing you already knew that."

Relief made it a little easier to breathe. Her mother was safe.

The relief was short-lived. There was still a long talk to be had. One that might or might not provide the answers she needed.

Javi pulled her into a hug then backed away quickly and glanced at Rich as though he still wasn't certain he trusted Dana's partner.

Her partner. Odd to start thinking of him as more than a nuisance. She was used to having her team, but in this situation? When she ought to be able to handle herself? The more she was around him, the more she had to admit he was right about having backup. Now, when she was about to face her mother, his presence was about her emotional well-being as well as her physical safety.

She swallowed her mounting anxiety and raised her big-girl deputy marshal facade. "This is Alex Richardson. Call him Rich." She aimed a finger at the young man she'd babysat years ago. "Javi Figueroa. He's a cop with the city." With formalities dispensed, she wanted to get this over with before anything happened to prevent her from obtaining answers. "Where's my mother?"

"In Mom's office." Javi grabbed her wrist as she moved to pass. "But Dana, seeing you is going to be a shock. She really does believe you're dead."

"Why?"

Javi started to speak, but then he shook his head. "Better if she tells you. I only know the little I overheard when she got here a few hours ago." He stepped aside.

Dana and Rich slipped past him and headed for the office. The kitchen was warm. The familiar scent of childhood Fridays spent in the restaurant—spices and tomatoes and sizzling meat—almost lulled her into comfort. The deepest, most frightened part of her wanted to stop, close her eyes and pretend this was a regular night from her childhood. Party night, maybe. When Christmas carols warbled from the karaoke machine and presents waited under the massive tree in the small lobby. When life was warm and innocent and safe.

But no. This was a time when emotions and sentimentality had to be shoved aside. At the office door, she paused and glanced over her shoulder at Rich, who dogged her steps. After what had happened to her at the house, there was no way he'd let her out of his sight.

It was a good thing. As much as she didn't want to need him, she certainly did. His presence was strength and calm in a world spinning out of control.

She straightened and shoved her feelings into a lockbox as she knocked on the door. "It's Dana."

Gasps rose from inside, then the door opened and arms pulled her into an embrace she recognized all too well.

Her mother.

Karen Santiago muttered in the rapid Spanish that tended to pour out when she was emotional. The comfort of her mother's arms and voice made Dana want to sink in and let the grown-ups fix all of her problems.

Except Karen was part of the problem. Possibly the *entire* problem.

Dana pulled away, glanced at Stephanie where she stood by her desk, then looked her mother in the eye. The connection nearly gave her vertigo. The woman she knew better than anyone else had suddenly become a perfect stranger.

Her mother reached for her. "I thought you were gone. I thought—"

Dana stiffened and backed away, colliding with Rich's chest.

Karen's face fell, but she quickly reset her expression to one of neutrality. "I wondered if you'd come."

No words would squeeze out past the building lump in Dana's throat. Seeing her mother piled everything on her. Her suspension. The lies her parents had told. The truth of whose blood ran through her veins. She sank into a chair and looked up at the woman she'd never questioned. The woman who'd rocked her when she was sick, who had let her cry on her shoulder when Andrew King stood her up for the homecoming dance and had prayed nightly over her at bedtime.

The woman who wasn't her mother, at least not in the way she'd always claimed.

On a hunch, Dana unrolled the plastic bag that held the knife and laid it on the desk beside where her mother stood. She cleared her throat. "Danna Marquez."

Karen stared at the knife. Her expression went blank. From her dark eyes to her full lips, there was no emotion, though her skin paled.

Maybe Dana was wrong. Maybe all of this was wrong. Maybe the DNA tests were inaccurate and she was Dana Santiago after all.

Her mother lifted her eyes and turned to Stephanie, who had yet to say a word. "Everybody leave. I need to talk to Dana alone."

When Rich shifted, Dana reached back and grabbed his wrist. "He stays." In a world without a compass, he had become the constant. The one person she could count on, who had yet to lie to her.

The one person she could trust.

There wasn't time to analyze how a stranger could become a part of her life so quickly. All Dana knew was she needed him beside her.

As the door closed behind Stephanie, Karen looked from Dana to Rich. The air was heavy with the aroma of comfort food and the stench of family tension. "Who is he?"

"No. Who am *I*? Who are *you*?"

"I'm your mother."

"DNA says otherwise." Dana didn't want to be cold or cruel, but grief drove her. Fear drove her. Hot and festering, it pushed from inside and spilled on the woman who'd hidden the truth.

Dana rocketed to her feet. "You've lied to me my whole life. Now, because of you, I have no job. I have no name. I have nothing." The words felt like shouts, but her ragged throat probably shredded them into harsh whispers.

A hand, warm yet firm, rested on her back.

Rich warning her, stabilizing her.

Dana's breaths came in giant heaves, washing cool air over her feverish emotions. "Why?" That was all she really wanted to know. There might be a good reason, but fear and pain clouded what that might be.

With a heavy sigh, her mother sank to the edge of the desk and stared at the. "I always meant to tell you, but every day made it harder. Like concrete, it grew harder until telling you…" Her hands fluttered, and she lifted her eyes to meet Dana's. Tears brimmed in the corners. "You decided to go into the Marshals Service. If they had known you were the child of Jairo and Rachel Marquez, they might not have—"

"They think I lied." The words were harsh whispers. "They think I knew and I hid the truth. I'm suspended pending an investigation and, unless I can prove otherwise, I'll be dismissed. Disgraced. Without my job, who am I? Better yet, who am I *now*?" There was the crux of it. The thing that made her feel as though her tether to the planet had snapped and she floated lost in space.

"You're my daughter."

Dana's head swiveled. The backs of her knees collided with the chair.

Rich's hand slipped to her waist, supporting her. He didn't let go, even when she righted herself.

"They obtained DNA from Jairo and Rachel." Dana jammed her index finger into her own chest, punctuating the words. "I am their daughter. Their blood is in my veins. That. Changes. Everything. Who I am, where I work, where I come from…" Her hand dropped to her side and bounced off her thigh. "Who am I?" She sank to the chair, spent, and buried her face in her hands.

She wouldn't cry.

Rich's hand slid to her shoulder as he continued to

offer silent support. His touch was the only thing that kept her from coming unglued. It made no sense. He was nobody to her.

Except he was.

Lighter, familiar hands rested on her knees as her mother knelt in front of her. "Birthing a child doesn't make you a mother. Siring a child doesn't make you a father. Jairo and—"

"Did you adopt me?" Maybe Rich was right earlier. She'd never considered how she came to be Dana Santiago. Only that she didn't know the truth. She lifted her head and met her mother's eyes, only inches from hers.

There was a hesitation, then an even slighter shake of the head. *"Mija..."*

The term of endearment did it. No matter what, this woman was her mom. She deserved respect. There had to be a reason she'd never told the truth. "I don't understand." Dana grasped her mother's hands, the cold wall around her heart cracking. "Just tell me one thing that's true."

"You were born Danna Marquez." Her mother held on as though she was afraid Dana might evaporate like mist through her fingers. "Your father and I kidnapped you."

TEN

"You kidnapped me from arms dealers?" Dana fought to keep her breaths steady as her heart rate surged. It was either an incredible act of love or sheer stupidity. "Why?"

Her mother's fingers slid up to her wrists, grasping tighter. "I don't want to cause you pain. Can't we stop there?"

"I need the truth." Dana couldn't be angry anymore. Couldn't work up the energy. She was shocked, exhausted…empty. "I need answers."

"Know I love you." Her mother's gaze wouldn't let go. "You believe me?"

"I guess." She pinched her lips together then drew a deep breath. "I want yesterday back." She felt like a five-year-old. Her confidence, her courage…it was all gone.

"If you could provide proof Dana didn't know…" Rich spoke for the first time since they'd walked into the restaurant. "There has to be something."

Her mother glanced up at the man who towered over both of them. She looked at Dana with a familiar raised eyebrow. *El novio?*

Dana's eyes drifted shut. Seriously? Her mother wanted to know if Rich was her boyfriend? She glanced over her shoulder at him—he had not left her side since this whole mess began. Heat rose in her cheeks. He probably knew enough Spanish to translate the question.

He was looking down at her, a slightly amused expression twitching the side of his mouth.

It was embarrassing, but it broke the tension. It also left a question she had no idea how to answer. *Boyfriend?* No. *Friend?* What did she call the person who'd put his life on the line when he didn't have to? Who held her and understood the things she couldn't process herself? "He's…" She shrugged. "He's Rich." Okay, that sounded bad. "His name's Rich. Not rich like he has a lot of money." At least, she assumed he didn't. She shook off his hand and the question. "Mom, the story?"

With a quick nod, her mother glanced at the chair next to Dana, and Rich moved it closer. She stood slowly, let go of Dana's wrists and slid onto the chair. "None of this will be easy, *mija*."

"It can't get any harder."

Her mother's expression said she wasn't sure, but she inhaled and squared her shoulders as though preparing for battle. "You were born in Argentina to Jairo and Rachel Marquez. Your real name is Danna Elena Marquez."

"You renamed me Dana Ellen." Close, but not too close.

"We didn't want to shock you too much. You were young, barely three when we brought you here."

"Why? Other than my parents were arms dealers."

Which was reason enough, but kidnapping the child of violent criminals didn't happen on a whim.

"Honestly, I'm really unsure why Rachel…" Her mother sighed and reached for Dana's hand. "She had no interest in being a mother. Jairo had none in being a father."

The pity in the words stung the backs of Dana's eyes, but she swallowed the hurt. "So what happened?"

"Dana, do not bury your pain. You cannot—"

"What happened?" There was no moving forward if she didn't *bury the pain.*

Karen pressed her lips together, staring at their locked fingers. "They hired me when you were born. I was the live-in nanny. Every feeding, every diaper change, your first words, I was there. You almost never saw Jairo or Rachel. Their interests were in the money and the power. Being parents never fit those things. Rachel believed that being a mother would make her seem weak, would make enemies run all over them. Maybe, in her own twisted way, she was protecting you. A rival cartel might have seen you as a target."

It was hard to feel for a woman as cold-blooded as Rachel Marquez, but something in Dana's heart squeezed. Her flesh-and-blood mother, who had carried her for nine months, hadn't wanted her. What did that make Dana? In the battle of nature versus nurture, what if she carried Rachel's nature deep inside?

"I met Ramon and married him. He wanted me to leave the Marquez family. They were dangerous, but they were never mean to me. I never saw them much, but they were well-known to be killers. I could not leave you. Until…" She shook her head. "Dana, it is enough to say that Ramon and I brought you here. That you are our child."

"It's not enough." Dana stood and brushed past Rich, staring at the dark wood door. She inhaled the scents of cilantro and beef. Tonight, the aroma was anything but comforting. It gave the world a feeling of déjà vu, of a past built on vapor. "I need to know everything. Otherwise, I have no idea who I am and no way to defend myself against charges that will cost me my job and reputation." Who in the tech world would hire someone without a security clearance? Someone the government had fired?

Behind her, Rich sniffed but said nothing.

What could he say? She should have asked him to leave, but she needed him near.

And she hated herself for it.

"Ramon and I, we knew of a man who could get us papers that said you were our daughter, papers that could get us into the United States. It cost us so much. Everything we had and more."

The words trailed off hesitantly. What *more*?

Dana whirled on her mother. "You stole from the Marquez family? Not just their daughter but their money?" That was suicidal. If Jairo and Rachel had figured everything out, it was no wonder fire rained down on Dana's and her mother's heads. "What were you thinking?"

"That I loved you." For the first time, her mother pulled herself to her full height. Her voice rose, carrying a force that made Dana step back. "Jairo and Rachel executed a man in front of you. You were three years old, and I knew in that moment that I could not let you stay there. One way or another, they would destroy you." Her voice finished on a jagged edge, and she stared at Dana with regret and a plea for understanding.

"My nightmares." Dana sank into the chair beside her mother. "They were real." The man, the gun, the blood…all real. Dana closed her eyes. She had to get a hold of herself or she was going to be sick. She'd seen a man murdered in cold blood as a child.

Her heart shattered for that child.

Anger toward her mother evaporated. Ramon and Karen Santiago had done nothing but love her. Had done nothing but see that she had the best life possible.

Even as she drew her mother close in a hug that spoke the forgiveness she couldn't, Dana glanced up at Rich. The truth healed her heart, but it did nothing to fix her life.

In his entire life, Rich had never wanted to hold a woman as much as he wanted to hold Dana Santiago. He clenched his fists and paced to the door to stop himself.

This was between Dana and her mother. He was a bodyguard.

Nothing more.

But if that was true, why did Karen Santiago's story break him? Right now, he was feeling things he hadn't felt in years. His heart ached in ways it hadn't since he'd walled his emotions off after Amber died.

Worse, why had he lost part of himself when Dana looked over her mother's shoulder at him?

The pain in her expression, the confusion layered behind the temporary relief of forgiving her mother. He wanted to hop the first plane to Argentina and confront the people who'd dared to hurt her as a child. He'd walk out the front door of this restaurant right now and take out anyone who dared try to hurt her again.

He'd die for her.

Not simply because he'd been asked to protect her. Because, from the moment they'd had their first real conversation, she'd made him *feel*. In hindsight, he could see what he couldn't see in the moment. He wasn't standing here because Wyatt had asked him to come on their mutual friend's behalf. He was here because he *chose* to be. Because something inside wouldn't let him be anywhere else.

The realization drove his mind into chaos. Planting both fists on the cool wood door, he rested his forehead against the grain and managed to hold himself together. He couldn't let Dana see what she'd done to him. There was too much chaos in her life, and she'd made it clear she had no room for any man.

Not that he should be entertaining such thoughts. He'd loved Amber and lost her. No way could he ever go through that kind of pain again. Plans were fragile things, easily broken, easily shattering him.

Dana's pain scraped against his raw emotions and did nothing but confirm the truth. The sooner they tucked her somewhere safe and he returned to his life without her, the better off they'd all be.

He cleared his throat. "I hate to interrupt…" Was his voice really husky? What in the world was this woman doing to him?

The women pulled apart, but he looked at Karen, not Dana. If he met her eye while his emotions ran rampant, the consequences could be disastrous in more ways than one. "How did you know you were in danger? Do you know who's behind all of this?"

"All of this?" Karen looked confused as she turned to Dana. "I thought Jairo and Rachel had found you. When you walked through the door, it was like seeing someone raised from the dead. I've been trying to call you, to email you."

"I left everything in North Carolina to avoid being tracked. I was attacked twice there and once in Georgia." When Karen gasped, Dana squeezed her mother's fingers. "I'm fine." She quickly related the past two days, including her suspension. She glossed over the severity of the attempts on her life. "When I saw the refrigerator, I came here."

"It was a vain hope you were alive." Karen covered their clasped hands with her free hand. "I noticed the same car follow me to work for two days. Since we ran from Argentina so many years ago, I have always noticed anything different. I have always been afraid the Marquez family would find us. I should have told you so you could watch your back, but with your job and with the fact you look nothing liked you did as a three-year-old, I assumed you were safe."

"You were followed?" Rich hated to be pushy, but the way things were going, they might have to run sooner rather than later. The last thing he wanted was to be caught off guard.

Karen glanced at him gratefully, a look he didn't fully understand. "Several times. I tried to call you, to see how Sam's wedding went, but no answer. When the man showed up, I got scared. And then when I came home from work this evening, he came to the house, tried to break in. I moved the pictures, escaped out the back and came here."

"This is why you had a plan all along, why you had the signal set up," Dana said.

Her mother nodded.

"Why not call the police?" It would have been the smart move.

Karen turned toward Rich. "I have never called the cops in my life. Have never had a traffic ticket, even. My identity, Dana's identity, they are all fake. I held my breath the whole time she was having background checks and secret clearance checks, certain we'd be found. If it is revealed who I am, they will discover I am not a legal American. Dana is, because Rachel was born here and met Jairo in college. They moved to Argentina when his father grew ill and could no longer run his organization. But me? No."

"Now what?" Dana stood and paced to the other side of the small office, away from Rich. "What will you do? You can't live in Stephanie's office. You can't stay without putting them in danger, too."

"*Mija*, there is so much you know nothing about. I am going into hiding until this blows over. My job thinks I am taking leave for a family emergency. I depart tonight." She stood and turned toward Dana. "You come, too."

There it was. The solution. Relief relaxed his tense muscles. Dana could go into hiding with her mother. She'd be safe. Rich stepped around the chair and stood beside Karen, a united front. "If she has someone who can safely hide you, then you should—"

"I already told you no." Dana whirled on him, her fists balled. "I need freedom to investigate. If I hide,

To get your 4 FREE REWARDS:
Complete the survey below and return the insert today to receive up to 4 FREE BOOKS and FREE GIFTS guaranteed!

"4 for 4" MINI-SURVEY

1 Is reading one of your favorite hobbies?
☐ YES   ☐ NO

2 Do you prefer to read instead of watch TV?
☐ YES   ☐ NO

3 Do you read newspapers and magazines?
☐ YES   ☐ NO

4 Do you enjoy trying new book series with FREE BOOKS?
☐ YES   ☐ NO

Please send me my Free Rewards, consisting of **2 Free Books from each series I select** and **Free Mystery Gifts**. I understand that I am under no obligation to buy anything, as explained on the back of this card.

☐ **Love Inspired® Romance Larger-Print** (122/322 IDL GQ5X)
☐ **Love Inspired® Suspense Larger-Print** (107/307 IDL GQ5X)
☐ **Try Both** (122/322 & 107/307 IDL GQ6A)

FIRST NAME	LAST NAME

ADDRESS

APT.#	CITY

STATE/PROV.	ZIP/POSTAL CODE

EMAIL ☐ Please check this box if you would like to receive newsletters and promotional emails from Harlequin Enterprises ULC and its affiliates. You can unsubscribe anytime.

LI/SLI-520-MS20

I can't clear my name. In fact, I look even guiltier."
She fixed her gaze on him. "Have you thought this
through? You're in this now, too. They know who you
are, *Espectro*." She practically spit the words. They
dripped with sarcasm that nearly overpowered the
room. "You're a target, too. I won't hide if you're out
there in the wind. I..." Her expression collapsed, but
she put it back together so fast, Rich wasn't entirely
sure he'd seen the flicker of weakness. "I won't leave
you out there alone. I can't."

The way she looked at him, the conviction and emotion in her voice—for a moment that dragged on longer
than he could calculate, they were the only two in the
room. Whatever had broadsided him moments earlier
had clearly hit her, too.

The air between them charged. Their hearts were
in as much danger as their lives. Neither was leaving
the other behind, but neither was free to express why.

Everything was hopeless.

Rich broke contact and turned to Karen, who
watched him with the same concerned-mother look
he'd received from Amber's mom more than once.
Given their current situation, it was completely out
of place.

Karen started to speak, but a rapid knock rattled
the door.

Javi, the young cop from the kitchen. His gaze
skimmed Rich then found Dana. "We have a problem."

ELEVEN

Dana jumped and spun. There was no time to process her mother's revelations.

Rich was already between her and the door. "What kind of trouble?"

Javi looked at him, then addressed Dana. Guess Rich still hadn't earned his trust. "Two guys pulled up in a late-model silver sedan. They're not regulars. Thomas thought he saw someone out back right before they came inside, but he didn't get a good look. They're sitting in the lobby. Said they're waiting for someone, but we close in half an hour, so..." He glanced over his shoulder. "They're watching the restaurant. Normally, I'd say it could be nothing, but given the circumstances, none of you can be too careful."

Rich watched the door. "Are they armed?"

"One guy has a knife in a sheath on his right hip. Didn't get a good look at the other."

Dana blew out an exasperated breath. What was the deal with these men and their knives? She nodded at Rich and then at the desk. When he unrolled the knife and laid it down, she pointed at it. "Does it look like one of those?" Her plan had been to ask her mother if she recognized the weapon, but time had run out.

"Near as I can tell." Javi strode to Dana's mother, who had glanced at the knife but had shown no reaction. "We need to push up the timeline and get you out of here. I've called. They can meet us sooner, but they won't wait around for you if you aren't there when we get there."

Dana flinched. Her mother had hired a human smuggler once to get them out of Argentina. She'd done it again tonight to get herself to safety. There were so many legal ramifications. So many things could go wrong. This wasn't WitSec. It was outlaws out to make a buck, and they'd sell out her mother to the highest bidder in a heartbeat. "Can we trust whoever you're handing her off to?"

Javi stiffened and stood taller. "This isn't a smuggler. This is a friend of Mama's. He used to work for the CIA. He'll get her to safety and hide her until this passes over."

"He'll hide Dana, too." Rich's gray eyes went steely. For him, there would be no more discussion.

There was no more discussion for her, either. She wasn't hiding, and there was nothing he could do about it. She was the one holding the car keys. "Unless you plan to sedate me, you already know how this is going to go down."

He opened his mouth and stepped forward, an argument on his lips, but Dana sliced the air with her hand. "We're done talking." She turned to Javi. "Get my mother out of here. Now."

It was the hardest order she had ever given. Her heart wanted to go with her mom, to protect her. Her mind said she was putting Javi and his family in the line of fire, but they were out of choices. She couldn't hide, not if she was ever going to put an end to this.

"Aaron is going to take her. I'm staying to watch the restaurant and to call in backup from the station if these guys so much as twitch their index finger in a way I don't like." Javi tossed her a set of keys. "Those are to the old pickup in the back garage. Nobody looking for you would have been able to see it. Mama said to take it in case they saw your rental." He reached for her mother's hand. "We have to go now. Thomas is keeping an eye on the men, and we had Aaron check outside. They're the only two in sight, so if we can get you out the back, we can get you to safety."

Dana's mother turned to her. There was strength in her gaze. "I know better than to argue when you are like this."

Dana rounded the desk and embraced the woman who had raised her, who had been Mama where her birth mother had failed. "When this is over, I'll come for you, but I have to stay on the outside if we ever want to be safe again."

"*We're* ending this." Rich's voice cut in, the emphatic, deep tone sending a warm shiver through Dana's stomach.

She didn't respond. She simply released her mother with a quick nod, a silent promise. *It will all be okay.*

Karen turned to follow Javi out the door, then stopped and reached into her pocket. She dropped a key into Dana's hand. "I have a locker at my gym. It's open all night. A-42. Your history is in there." With one last look tinged with a hint of longing, she turned and rushed out the door behind Javi.

Dana turned to Rich as the door closed behind her. There was no time for tears or sentiment. They had to get moving.

Rich was staring at the door. He pivoted slowly to face her. "Why do I feel like I somehow stepped into a well-oiled family of spies?" He waved his hand toward the door. "Contingency plans, safe houses, some shadowy network of…something?"

"Stephanie, who owns this place, is a widow. She was married to Chad, a former CIA operations officer. I have no idea how long Stephanie's known, but I'm guessing Chad had contingencies for his family that are being set into place tonight for mine." She shoved away from the desk and grabbed the knife. "I didn't wind up working in WitSec by accident. I grew up so close to this family they were like my own. It was practically in my DNA." No, not her family, and not her DNA. Her DNA was tainted by murder and corruption. Her DNA belonged to the very criminals she protected others from.

"I'm guessing you have your own contingency plans?"

"My job isn't as covert and dangerous as Bill's probably was. I never thought I had a need." No. She'd never imagine she'd have to run for her life because her whole existence was a lie. The weight of revelation, the stress of running and the fear for her mother settled on her with palpable weight.

Rich reached for her but didn't touch her. "We need to get you to some place where you can take a minute to process."

"No. The way I see it, right now, we have two choices." She grabbed the plastic-wrapped knife from the desk and held it up by the handle. "We can slip out and let these guys vanish into the wind, or..." Let's see how well Rich really knew her.

His eyebrow arched, and he seemed to shake whatever weird vibe he'd been carrying since they walked into the office. "Or we confront them now when they aren't aware we know they're here."

"We get answers by hitting them head on."

Rich reached for the doorknob. "What do you say we have a chat with Javi about holding off on backup until we need it and then go wait by their car?"

"I say, 'After you.'"

Rich leaned against the hood of the silver sedan, arms folded over his chest and ankles crossed in front of him. It was a stupid pose, really. His best attempt to look casual while waiting for the men chasing Dana to emerge from the crowded restaurant. Normally, he had no trouble blending into his surroundings. It was a skill he'd cultivated in Special Forces first and then had honed on the Mountain Springs Police Department.

But Dana had spun him off his game. He was better than this goofball he'd become, a man who couldn't even figure out what do to with his own hands. All because, two cars away, Dana stood watch. He could practically feel her eyes on him, and it turned him into an awkward preteen all over again.

He'd only agreed to her plan if she stayed out of the way and didn't reveal herself unless things went sideways and he needed backup. No need to put herself in danger by showing her face prematurely.

She'd wanted to be the bait, but he had to draw the line somewhere. His job was to protect her. He would not put her in harm's way. All they needed was for the men to admit who they worked for. If they did, Rich could pass the intel to Isaiah and get to work from the top down instead of them continuing to run for their lives.

Then he could walk away from Dana and this ridiculous feeling putting down uncomfortable roots in his chest.

That part of the plan grew less appealing with every passing second. Proof he needed to get away from Dana and back to the real world as fast as he possibly could.

The door swung open, leaking light and laughingly sung karaoke into the parking lot. Rich straightened, but it wasn't his target. A man and a woman walked hand in hand across the gravel lot, their arms and sides close, heads bent toward one another.

The man spoke. The woman laughed. They shared a quick kiss, then left together in a red sedan.

They made it look so easy.

Back in the day, it *had* been easy. He'd had that relationship. Those quick kisses and easy moments, so effortlessly taken for granted.

Yeah, he'd had everything. Before he'd let a murderer reach Amber. Before he'd felt his dreams die in his arms.

Dreams were short-lived creatures. Never again could he let himself—

The door opened again. Two men exited. They walked in his direction but watched the parking lot as though searching. The tall one had a knife at his hip. The other wore an empty sheath and walked with a slight limp.

Gotcha. Adrenaline poured into Rich's system, his fight-or-flight response choosing to fight.

The moment they spotted him, their steps slowed. The tall one muttered something to his partner, then reached for his knife, although he didn't extract it.

Yet.

Dana had better be in position with a clean line of sight. And Stephanie had better be good at keeping all of the patrons inside the restaurant until this confrontation was over. His biggest fear at the moment, next to Dana dying due to some slipup on his part, was an innocent getting caught in the cross fire.

"Fellas." He stood and held his arms out to the sides, the plastic-wrapped knife in one hand. "I think I have something you might want back."

Tall Guy's expression hardened with the kind of hatred Rich hadn't seen since his last firefight overseas. A quick flash of death and blood and screams made him waver on his feet, but only for an instant. These men couldn't see him off his game. They'd take advantage before he could recover his footing.

"You are a brave one." Short Guy was clearly the leader. He tipped a quick nod to his partner, and they eased slowly apart, one to Rich's right and one to his left, though they maintained their distance. "There are two of us and one of you." He let his gaze drift before bringing it back to Rich. "Unless she is hidden somewhere and waiting for a chance to strike?"

"She's long gone. Left with her mother."

To his left, Tall Guy cursed under his breath then muttered something that ended with *muerta.*

Dead.

"Yet here you are. Why would you confront us if

your girlfriend is safely hidden?" Short Guy's hand rested on his knife, but he still didn't withdraw it. Likely, he saw value in keeping Rich alive. Probably for information.

Would they torture him if they took him? The way the terrorists had tortured Fitz?

Again, Rich had to force himself back into the present, away from the stench of the past. He wrestled his voice into submission, level and hard. "She's not my girlfriend. I was assigned to keep her safe. But now I know who you are. Where you come from. Who issued the order for you to come for her." It was a huge guess, one he hoped was close enough to the mark to spook them.

"I doubt that very seriously."

"Never doubt." Rich lifted the knife higher and leveled a knowing gaze on the younger man to his left. "You left your business card behind. I'm sure a lot of people in some pretty high places would be really unhappy with you for being so careless with incriminating evidence."

Tall Guy whipped toward his partner and closed the gap between them. He grabbed the younger man by the arm and spoke in rapid Spanish, the angry words a verbal beating accompanied by sharp gestures toward Rich.

Spanish wasn't his strong suit. He hadn't had a single lesson since high school, but he sure could interpret the tone and the actions. This was a smackdown of epic proportions.

Divide and conquer. Point for Team Dana.

"If you're interested in a deal—" he raised his voice above the tirade "—I might be persuaded to return it."

The man broke off in midsentence and turned to Rich, resuming his position slightly to the right. "For what price?"

"For the right money, this could go back to you and I could forget I ever saw it. For the even more right price, I could be persuaded to tell you where your target is hiding. Save you both from a worse fate than... Well, you know."

"Or I could kill you and take it." This time, Short Guy drew his knife and held it low.

Rich pulled out his pistol and aimed at the man's chest. With his left hand, he held the knife toward its owner. "You're not faster than a bullet, buddy." His voice shifted from friendly to deathly deep. "Either of you so much as flinches, I put a bullet in you and I re-acquaint your friend with his knife in a very personal way. You understand?" He prayed the men obeyed.

With a snarl, the man sheathed his knife and lifted his hands slightly. "I keep my knife. If I return without it..."

He didn't need to finish the sentence. The implication of death was the very reason his buddy's face was still pale.

"I am guessing it is not truly money you are after. You have dogged Danna Marquez's steps, protecting her from us and from our men. Money will not easily buy you off. What is it you really want?"

"Information."

Stony silence from both men.

Fine. He could play their way, but not for long. It was only a matter of time before someone exited the restaurant. "What's the endgame?"

There was a shuffle behind him. Short Guy's gaze

shifted over Rich's shoulder. "I do not need to answer your questions, because you are not in charge here."

"I would put the weapon down if I were you." A new voice—a deeper male voice—came from over Rich's right shoulder.

Rich's insides collapsed, taking his breath with them even as he tried to keep his voice passive. He'd definitely been flanked.

The voice again. "I would take a look, friend. Because we have what we came for. Now you are expendable."

"Rich, don't listen to him."

Dana. He glanced to the side.

A broad-shouldered man stood out of reach, one arm around Dana's waist...

Holding a knife to her throat.

TWELVE

Stupid.

Dana held herself stiff, trying to keep the cold blade of the knife from slicing into the delicate skin at her throat.

These guys were immensely stupid if they thought she would surrender so easily. If they thought she was a weak woman who would go down without a fight.

Not. Going. To. Happen.

Her gaze met Rich's. He hesitated, an unreadable look in his eye, then dipped his head in a quick nod.

Yep. Everyone was in place.

Rich split the air with an ear-piercing whistle.

As he did, Dana raised her foot and brought it down hard on her captor's instep. She drove her elbow into his diaphragm and stepped backward hard against him as his grips on her and on his knife loosened. Then she shoved his arm away, and the knife clattered to the ground. Drawing her pistol, she stood over the man just out of leg's reach and held him at bay.

The scene devolved into controlled chaos. Rich dived at the shorter guy to his right while Javi leveled his weapon on the unarmed man to Rich's left. In seconds, both were subdued.

Like clockwork.

The man on the ground before her glared with a gaze that could melt diamonds as he cursed her entire family.

She wasn't sure which family. Dana kept her face impassive. "On your stomach."

For a second, he acted as though he wasn't going to comply. Dana lifted the pistol so it aimed right between his eyes.

That seemed to supply the proper motivation. As efficiently as she could in the narrow space between vehicles, she zip-tied his hands and ankles with the restraints Javi had provided and stepped back.

The other two assailants were likewise restrained on the ground behind the cars.

In the distance, sirens wailed.

Javi held his pistol over the men and cast a quick look at Dana. "You two get out of here. Mom and I will make sure the cops handle these three."

Dana was already backing away, but Rich hesitated. "They won't ask questions?"

Javi smiled. "Mom once trussed up two would-be armed robbers and had them in custody before the call ever went out to the police. They won't ask too many questions. Besides, these are my people. I'll take care of this, and I'll be sure to do a thorough interrogation once we get them booked. You get out of here."

Dana tapped Rich on the shoulder. "Let's go." If the police showed up, Dana and Rich would be tied up all night answering questions. Right now, their only known pursuers were subdued. Given time, more might descend on Oswego and bring war with them. She wanted to get the information from her mother's gym locker and leave town before that happened.

In the back garage, she unlocked the blue-and-white Ford pickup and climbed into the driver's seat, then narrowly made it out of the parking lot before the police arrived. It was all she could do not to shove the gas pedal to the floor. Never had time been such a precious commodity, not even on the many missions she'd been involved with during her WitSec field days.

Beside her, Rich silently watched her navigate the streets at only a couple of miles an hour over the speed limit. He'd said nothing since her appearance in the parking lot. He seemed a little pale, even though everything had gone perfectly to plan and had drawn out the third member of the hit team, the one they'd guessed was there all along.

It was almost as though he was seeing something that wasn't there. As if the evening had rattled him. As if he'd thought she was truly in danger of being murdered.

Murdered.

Oh no. Her fingers dug into the cracked vinyl steering wheel. His fiancée.

She'd lived her worst nightmare as a child over and over again in her dreams, but Rich had watched his play out in reality. Tonight had to have been a reminder of the most horrific moments he'd ever endured. "Rich?"

"Hmm?" He shook his head, seemed to come back from somewhere else. "What?"

"I…" What could she say? Apologizing would only rub salt in the wound, forcing him to talk about a time in his life he probably had no desire to relive. "Any preferences on a place to bunk down for a few days? Worse comes to worse, we can pick up some camping gear and head into the Adirondacks. It's cold, but it wouldn't be the first time either of us has had to suffer for the job."

"I actually have a better idea."

"Do tell."

"I have a buddy I served with who has a place up in the Thousand Islands region. He's separated from the military, but his wife's stationed at Fort Drum. While you were setting up your plan back there with Javi and Stephanie, I texted him and gave him the basics. He's open to us taking refuge at his place."

"I don't know." The words leaked out slowly. The last thing she wanted to do was put more innocent people in danger. While Stephanie and her crew were experienced, it still gnawed at Dana that they'd had to get involved. "I hate to put civilians at risk."

Rich chuckled, but it wasn't with amusement. "Webster is anything but a civilian."

"Meaning…?"

"Meaning you have super-secret-squirrel people in your pocket, and I have some in mine."

Okay then. So the guy was a hard-hitting GI Joe type like Rich. Possibly something more. This could work. "Thousand Islands is only about ninety minutes from here. Think that's enough distance?" Even if Javi could convince his counterparts to keep their pursuers busy for the next day or so, she wanted to be far out of reach of them and anyone on the other end of their one phone call.

"Webster's living on land his family's owned for al-

most as many years as America has been a country. He
literally has his own island in the St. Lawrence River."

Impressive. They'd vacationed in the Thousand Islands a few times when she was a kid. She'd always
been fascinated by the hundreds of islands dotting the
St. Lawrence Seaway, some with a house or two and a
few with small farms and even cows. Most were vacation homes, but for their purposes tonight? "Difficult
to access, easy to defend…"

"Plus, your hosts will be a former Special Forces
operator–turned–overseas security contractor married to a combat helicopter pilot. I think we can all
handle the situation."

She sure hoped he was right.

"They're expecting us," he said. "Webster will meet
us and help us hide the truck, then ferry us to the island from his private dock. We should be able to lie
low there for as long as we need."

It was the best plan they had. It sounded so close to
perfect, Dana wasn't sure she trusted it.

But she had unfinished business only a couple of
miles away before she could even think about heading out of town. "I'm making a stop at Mom's gym."

"Is that safe? I know you want answers, but—"

"I don't want them. I *need* them. My mother could
testify that I had no idea who I really was, but she's in
hiding for the duration. Without what's in her locker,
I have nothing." She slowed the truck for a stoplight,
then reached across the seat and gripped his hand. "I
have to know where I came from."

"You already know."

"It's all this vague dream, Rich. I feel like I haven't
lived in reality in days." Her fingers tightened around

his. "Maybe, if I see it in black and white, everything will be real. I can move forward and get to the bottom of this. Find out where those men are from and make this all stop. With proof, I can go to WitSec, get my clearances back and convince someone to launch a real investigation. Regain my credibility. Regain *myself*."

"You are the same Dana Santiago I first met last year and I got to know better this past week. Where you came from doesn't change you."

The low timbre of his voice forced her to look at him. In the red glow from the stoplight, he watched her with a different intensity than before. As the light shifted to green, he squeezed her hand then let go. "You're still a tough-as-nails federal agent."

"Only if I can prove I didn't knowingly tell a lie. Otherwise? I'm nobody."

"So, you have a lot of blanks to fill in if you want to stay here." Corey Webster's grin belied the harsh words. He tossed a block of sandpaper to Rich across the wood hull of the boat in his garage workshop.

The heady, comforting scents of coffee and fresh sawdust hung in the air. The early morning was chilly on the small island, but, inside the shop, it was warm and messy, exactly like a guy's space ought to be. "Plus, it's going to take some muscle from you to earn your keep."

"Sure it is." For the first time since he'd walked out of the barn at Sam and Amy's wedding, Rich relaxed in the company of someone who understood. Webster had been his battle buddy in basic training at Fort Benning many years earlier. The forced togetherness had bonded them instead of dividing them. They'd served together again at Fort Bragg, and Webster had been on the fateful mission when Fitz was tortured and murdered by insurgents.

There were only a handful of men who'd survived the nightmare. They all bore physical and emotional scars no one else understood. Although Web had been single when their team's spouses and girlfriends were attacked on home soil after their return, he'd felt the pain of each death, had even rushed into a burning house on a rescue mission.

So much had changed in a few years. Rich had lost Amber in that horrible season when his body and mind were still recovering from the attack and Fitz's death.

Webster had declared his intent to remain single after all of the bloodshed. Two months later, he'd met Emily, a hard-core combat chopper pilot. They'd married within weeks. Web left the military to work on missions so deep, Rich didn't have the clearance level to be read in. Emily flew with the combat aviation brigade at Fort Drum. Rather than live on post, they'd settled in the onetime vacation home that had been in Web's family for generations.

Apparently, his buddy also built boats. Rich ran his hand along the smooth wood hull of what would eventually be a two-seater canoe. "She's gorgeous."

Web stopped sanding and rested a hand lovingly on the cedar. "We'll see. It's a bigger project than I thought it'd be. If she floats, I'll build another. If she sinks…" He twisted his lips together and studied a seam. "Well, I've got so much money in her, I guess I'll haul her up from the bottom and rebuild her. Em would have my head if I did anything less, even though the whole thing was her idea."

Rich laid the block of sandpaper to the wood and went to work, taking satisfaction in watching rough wood turn smooth under grit and pressure. "Your wife suggested you dump a literal boatload of money into this thing?"

"Ha-ha. I forgot what a funny guy you are." Web's voice was flat, but he smiled. It was a more mature smile than Rich had ever seen in him. "I think Em got tired of me keeping her up at night with the pacing and the nightmares, so she figured I'd do better out here. She was right. When I can't sleep, I work on the boat. The memories get to be too much, I work on the boat." He stopped and ran his palm over a plank, his eyes following the motion of his hand. "I don't hear Fitz screaming in my sleep so much anymore."

Rich didn't react, just kept up the rhythmic motion of sanding with the grain. Too many nights, sleep had come hard. When it had come, he'd found himself bolting up, convinced he could hear Fitz's tortured howls. After Amber was murdered, the two events blended into a terrifying mash-up nightmare. There had been whole stretches of days when he hadn't slept until he'd passed out. Suicide had been a real and scary urge, stronger than he cared to confess.

Especially at night.

Rich ran his thumb over a rough spot and chased it with the sandpaper. "I went to a retreat. Barnes talked me into it. Colorado. Fishing. I don't know, something about being in fresh air that wasn't the stale air of my house…" He'd like to say the nightmares had totally gone away, but at least he'd come back with a new source of hope and a deeper walk with Jesus. There was more to the world than death. Even though he dared dream no personal dreams, having the retreat center to focus on had given him something positive to think about and plan for in the oh-dark-thirty hours that used to be his worst times.

"Now you're going to do the same for other wounded warriors."

"I hope so."

"Hmm." Web reached behind him, grabbed fresh sandpaper off the workbench and inspected it in greater detail than was necessary. "You planning to do it alone?"

"I've got investors lined up. A board. Some local pastors and counselors who've agreed to—"

"I'm not talking about business." For the first time since they'd started the deep conversation, Web caught Rich's eye. "I'm talking about you moving forward. Not trying to be a lone wolf who doesn't need anybody."

The comment grated on Rich's nerves, but he worked hard not to show it. Web had no idea what he was talking about. Sure, he'd been there when Fitz died, but when wives and girlfriends were dying at the hands of someone they'd trusted, Web had been single. He had no idea the pain or the terror that came from having his future die in his arms. Rich chose to ignore the real meaning behind Web's comment, the one about relationships and the future. "I have an entire police department of guys behind me, and most of them have volunteered to help. It's a small town, but we're a—"

"I don't hear you talking about friends." Web laid the sandpaper on the boat hull and braced his hands wide on the wood, eyeing Rich. "Ever since Amber died, you've held everybody at arm's length. You don't socialize."

"I'm talking to you right now, aren't I?" Rich laid his block down with a gentleness he definitely wasn't feeling. "You know, I haven't seen you in a few years, and this is how you want to talk to me?"

"That's what I mean. I call, you don't answer. You fire back one- and two-word texts that sound more like you're talking to a wrong number. I send emails, and you don't respond at all. For all we've been through, you've crawled into a hole. I don't hear from you in forever until you need a place to hide." He held up his hand, palm out. "It's good. We can go decades and not talk, and I'll still have your back. But you can't do this alone."

None of what Web was saying needed to be dignified with a response. Rich picked up his sandpaper and went back to work. "So how's married life other than Em kicking you out of the house?"

The only sound for a good minute was sandpaper on wood. It seemed Web wasn't going to answer, but then he huffed out a loud breath and went back to work. "Good. Better than single life. Better than I figured it would be. I jumped in fast, but that's how it had to be for me, I guess."

Maybe if he'd jumped into marriage faster with Amber. Yeah, he couldn't play the what-if game anymore. There was no *if.* He'd loved Amber and had lost her. Had grieved her and, while the pain would always sting, he had moved forward into life without her. He was living again but on his terms.

"So tell me about Dana. You can't show up at a man's house with someone who might be a fugitive and not give up the story. After all, she's in the kitchen having coffee with my wife. That's a lot of trust I'm offering."

Rich relaxed with the conversational heat off himself and gave a skeleton outline of the past few days. "All she wants is her life back, but it's never going to be what it was before this started." She was forever changed, even though she might not realize it. It seemed Dana had come to the conclusion that getting her job back would also restore her identity. That was going to be a lot harder than she realized.

"So you walked away from your life and put yourself in the line of fire for a stranger?" The tone of the question spoke more than the words did. The real question was, *What deeper feeling are you harboring for this woman?*

Rich didn't look up. He didn't know the answer himself.

Web leaned back, stretched, then returned to his work. "Are you ever going to let yourself love again?"

"Nope."

"That was abrupt."

"No reason to. I loved. I lost. I learned my lesson."

"Lesson?"

Guess they were having this conversation as the price he paid to keep Dana safely hidden. "I can't control tomorrow. I had my future mapped out. I had plans. I was happy. It all got ripped away. I'm good on my own with the retreat center. I'll let the rest of you risk your futures to God's whims." He winced. That wasn't how he really felt, was it?

"Harsh, brother." The sound of sandpaper stopped. Web sat back on the stool where he'd been resting, probably because his leg ached too much for him to stand on it too long. More than one insurgent's bullet had ripped through his calf on the day Fitz died. "Bad things happen all of the time. Doesn't mean you stop living. You're still alive. Must be a reason."

"I live. I live hard. In the past two years I've lived harder than I wanted to."

"Protecting other men's women and now this one. Ever think there might be something there?"

His sandpaper stuttered on the wood, but then Rich went back to work. "You gone back to school for psychology or something?"

"Church. God. Bible." Web tapped his head with his index finger. "I got me some of that wisdom the Proverbs are always talking about."

Rich cleared his throat to keep from cracking a smile at Web's exaggerated hillbilly drawl, perfectly timed to take the sting out of the conversation. "'Bout time."

"You still in love with Amber?"

Amusement…gone. "I'll always love Amber. I'll always wish she hadn't…" He stared at a spot over Web's head where a large metal Harley-Davidson sign took up most of the wall. "I grieved her. Hard. Part of her will always be with me. Part of me will always miss her, but if you're thinking the reason I haven't opened up to somebody else is because of her, then you're wrong." He exhaled roughly. "I never want to hurt like that again."

"Want my opinion?"

"Not really." Knowing Web, he'd get it anyway.

"I was watching when you came in last night. There's more between you and Dana than you want there to be." Web sliced the air with his hand, cutting off any argument Rich might work up. "You keep *almost* touching her. *Almost* looking at her. And she's doing the same with you."

"You have no idea what you're talking about."

"I don't?" Web's eyebrow arched. "I'm the man who met his match in a helicopter pilot and married her a month later because I *knew.* It made no sense to anyone else, but it did to us. Let go of the lie that you only get one dream. Let yourself live. Amber was a beautiful part of your story with a tragic, awful ending, but she wasn't your *whole* story." Web went back to work. "A man without a dream might as well be dead."

THIRTEEN

Dana shivered and drew the fleece jacket she'd borrowed from Emily tighter around herself, careful not to let the small metal box on her lap slide into the water below. The night air at the end of the Websters' boat dock was December iced and river damp. A nearly full moon cast enough light for her to see without a flashlight, although reading what might be in the box was out of the question. It would be dangerous to stay in the cold for long, but she'd needed to be alone with the truths her mother had hidden for so many years.

Dotted along the river and the shoreline, Christmas lights twinkled in homes and yards. It had been years since she'd slowed down enough to notice them. It was true she typically went to work and returned home again without ever seeing the outside. *Slowing down* wasn't in her vocabulary. Criminals didn't take holidays. The witnesses she protected needed her at her station, tracking down threats on their lives.

Yet her entire team had taken half of the last week off for Sam's wedding. He was going to be gone two weeks on his honeymoon. Other law enforcement officers across multiple agencies spent time with their families during the holidays.

To her knowledge, WitSec still hummed along without her. Was that a good or a bad thing? She needed the job, but did the job need her?

Obviously not, since *the job* had unceremoniously kicked her out. Dana huffed out a breath. The day had been long. She wasn't used to sitting still. There was little she could investigate from here. Nothing she could pursue unless she managed to dig up some leads. She'd landed in the exact place she'd tried to avoid— in hiding, trapped, with zero progress on determining who was trying to kill her.

Hopefully, there was something in the box to lead her to a next step.

If she could talk herself into opening it. As long as it remained locked, it contained all of the answers she needed. Once she lifted the lid, there was no going back. She'd either make peace with her past and find proof to clear herself, or she'd forever hover between the Dana she thought she was and the Danna she'd never imagined she'd be.

Footsteps thunked on the deck, echoing off the water below.

She didn't have to turn to know who it was. The stride was one she'd learned well over the past few days. Rich had come looking for her.

That was either an incredible annoyance or a disturbing comfort.

"Want some company?" He stopped somewhere behind her, probably realizing at the last second she'd come out here seeking solitude.

She'd felt rude hiding out in the guest room, so

she'd spent the day with Emily. Rich and Web had been in and out from the shed in the backyard, smelling more like lacquer and sawdust with every entrance and exit. Supposedly, they were working on some kind of boat, but she'd guess there was more talking than actual working.

"I can go back to the house…" It was the first time she'd ever heard uncertainty in his voice. It reminded her of a little boy hoping he wouldn't be picked last for kickball.

"You can stay. I'm just out here in the quiet. The house was getting too cooped up."

"I understand." He bent his knee and sat beside her, his thigh a mere inch from hers, close enough to feel the warmth he brought with him from the heated interior of the house. He leaned closer and tapped the box in her lap. "You open it yet?"

"No. I was thinking about it. What if…what if it's all meaningless to me? I want to at least remember something other than…"

"Other than what?"

Other than the nightmare she didn't want to air. She needed a minute and grasped at the first non-Dana thought in her head. "I noticed Web limps."

Rich settled back on his hands and stared at the stars. He considered them for a long time before he spoke. "He was in the same incident overseas as me. I caught a bullet in the shoulder. He caught more than one in the leg. He almost lost it. Actually not sure how he didn't."

"What happened?" Dana set the box aside and mimicked Rich's posture, leaning back to angle her head toward the sky. It felt as though all they'd ever talked about was her. Something deep inside her wanted to know more about him.

His head swiveled toward her. "We're not out here freezing to death because of me."

No, they weren't. What she wouldn't give for it not to be about her, either.

And, to be honest, not about searching for a memory that wasn't coated with violence.

Couldn't she have one happy impression? One thing connecting her to the young girl she hadn't known existed?

Rich shifted and sat straighter, resting his hand on her lower back as though he could feel her inner turmoil. "You okay?"

"Want to know the only thing I can remember about being a little kid, and I thought was just a nightmare until yesterday?"

"Sure." His hand was warm and his fingers squeezed lightly, encouraging her to share.

Unburdening herself to this man felt natural, right. Like the release she'd been searching for. "There's a courtyard, with grass and flowers and trees. There's a man on his knees, begging, uttering the words *I'm sorry*, over and over." Pain twisted in her gut, and Rich slipped closer, his arm encircling her shoulders. "Another guy stands above him with a gun pressed to the man's forehead." She tried not to whimper, although the urge was inside her, animalistic and almost unstoppable. "A woman with long dark hair—it's up in this elaborate…" She waved her hand over her hair, not quite able to find the words to describe it. "They're dressed so elegantly. There must have been some sort of party. She looks at the man with the gun and tells him to be a man. So he pulls the trigger." *So much blood.*

It was no nightmare. Her parents had killed a man in front of her. She shuddered. Their blood was her blood. Their DNA was her DNA.

"I'm right here. You don't have to do this alone." Rich's voice was deep and husky, and his arm around her shielded her. The dark edges of the vision faded.

She'd never wanted to lean on a man before, to let him hold her up. But here she was, seriously contemplating snuggling against him. Rich might be the only safe place she had left.

Problem was, they lived two separate lives. There was no room for him in her world, no way to do her job and fit him in. And Rich already had a great love, one she couldn't compare to. Dana inched away until his hand fell to the rough wood behind her, severing the connection.

But he was also her friend, and despite everything, she wanted him near while she plumbed the depths of a past she couldn't remember. Anchoring the box to her lap with one hand, she leaned to the side and pulled the key from her pocket, then inserted it into the small lock on the box. "Here goes..."

She twisted the key and lifted the lid on its hinges. The box was nearly empty except for a small stack of papers. She pulled them free as Rich slid the box away then activated the flashlight on his phone.

Dana angled the papers in the moonlight. The top one was a birth certificate. She squinted and ran her index finger over the name. "Danna Elena Marquez. Not Dana Ellen Santiago." If she'd expected her birth name to resurrect long-forgotten memories, she was wrong. The name meant nothing. "My birthday is not on October 17 It's March 12." The back of her eyes stung. She rubbed the corner of her left one. Hopefully, Rich wouldn't notice. "Not even my birthday is mine." There was no longer anger, just numbness tinged with sadness and deep-seated fear. What if she never found herself again?

There were some childhood drawings. A handful of official documents she didn't recognize. That was all. Nothing to prove she hadn't lied. Nothing to give her a clue to her own personality. "I guess I was expecting too much out of a metal box. I'll have to wait until it's safe for my mother to speak up on my behalf."

"I'm sorry." Rich retrieved the box and slid the papers into it. "Now what? We can—" He lifted the box and tilted it into the light from his phone. "There's a paper stuck in the lid." He turned it toward her. "It might be a picture."

Dana dipped her chin, her heart pounding, then carefully pried the item from the metal crease holding it captive. Her fingers shook. She flipped the photo over. A small toddler stared up at her, so tiny and innocent, laughing with the abandon only a child could feel. In the background, booths stretched along a midway, the signs in colorful Spanish. But it was the tiger clutched in the child's embrace that caught Dana's attention. Her heart stuttered. "Tito."

Rich leaned closer, his hand on her back and his head next to hers. "Who's Tito? You have a brother?"

Dizziness swirled the photo, either from the flood of memories or from the masculine warmth of the man who'd invaded her personal space. She swallowed a lump in her throat that could have been caused by either. "Tito. He was…he was my stuffed tiger. I must have…left him behind? I remember." She turned her head, excitement coursing through her. "Rich, I remember!"

His head was beside hers, so close their foreheads brushed as she turned. Her breath caught. Close enough to tilt her head and let her lips brush his.

He pulled away quickly, his hand dropping from her back. "What do you remember?"

It took her a second to catch her breath in the chill he left behind. "It's not much." But it was enough. "My father, Ramon, the man who raised me. We were at a carnival and he won Tito. It's the vaguest remembrance, more of a feeling, but this picture… I'm happy. Happy with my parents. The ones who raised me." She couldn't pull her eyes from the picture. "They saved me. They took me from that life. What would I have become if they hadn't?"

The crushing fear of what might have been stole her breath. Would she still have morals? Would she have bucked her family's criminal dealings? Or was her flight from Argentina God's way of protecting her?

Rich's hand reached for her, hovered. Web's words spun in his brain. *You keep almost touching her. And she's doing the same with you.*

It wasn't that he kept *almost* anything. He had touched her to offer help, to offer support.

Because he couldn't bear to watch her hurt. When pain marred her features, he felt it to his core. Every time. He wanted to be the man who made it all go away. He wanted to rescue her, whether she wanted him to or not.

The truth exhilarated him and nauseated him at the same time, scrambling his thoughts. Truthfully, he was past thinking. For the first time in years, he was feeling. Truly feeling.

It was terrifying.

Rich set the small box aside, angled his body toward Dana and wrapped his arms around her.

She stiffened then nestled into his chest, warm yet shivering. She'd been through so much. Faced so much uncertainty. How could he make it all better?

He couldn't. But he could be here now, as she processed the heights of joy and the depths of pain and the questions about her future, about her identity. "Even if you'd been raised in Argentina, I have to believe you'd still be you. Somehow, the Dana God created would have survived, would have still been a woman of integrity and character." *And bravery and beauty.*

"How?"

Words tickled the edges of his memory. Something a preacher had said at his cousin's baptism. "Web said something about a psalm in the Bible. Maybe 139? It talks about putting you together in your mother's womb. He knew who your mothers would be, Dana. The one who bore you and the one who raised you."

She sniffed and settled heavier against his chest, drawing an ache from deep inside him, a longing he'd never felt before. He almost groaned under the weight of it. Dipping his head, Rich rested his cheek against her hair. He could press a kiss there, but something stopped him.

Something deeper. Something more that needed to be said. More from the psalm he'd read this afternoon after his talk with Web. He'd felt God's urging in the past, but it had been so long ago. Right now, the nudge said Dana needed to hear his words more than he needed to hold her close.

"It also says He knew all of your days before you were born. He wrote them down. He knew what would happen to you. He knew who your parents would be and what they would do, and He made a way ahead of time for Ramon and Karen to raise you. Maybe they went about it the wrong way, but God made a way for you to be you. He set it all up..." The words died as God dropped truth into his spirit.

If He'd made a plan and a path for Danna Marquez to become Dana Santiago, then He'd prepared all of Rich's days, too. *All* of them. Even the days when suffering and death tinged his memories bloodred.

God had prepared Fitz's days and Amber's days also. He knew how their lives would end from their very beginning. Though God hadn't caused Amber's death, He'd allowed it. Why had it ended so horribly for both of them?

Because they had their own books, their own purposes, their own writings from God. Stories Rich would never understand but that he had to trust were important and real.

She was part of your story. You're still here...

He was still here. He still had a story to be written. It was time he picked up the pen and started putting down words. "We all have a story." The whisper was rough and broken, heavy with truth.

Dana shifted and edged slightly away, though she stayed in his arms. "What's yours? What happened to you and Web?"

How did she know that was the story that had

started it all? The one that opened fissures in his soul that carved into canyons when Amber died? He'd ceased to be himself long before a murderer stole her life. Amber had tried to talk about his anger more than once, about the raging grief and pain that had driven his emotions in a wild gallop. She'd hesitated when he'd asked her to marry him, probably because she wasn't sure who he was anymore and likely because she knew his proposal was a desperate grasp for stability.

Somehow, Dana knew there was a story he needed to tell.

Somehow, Rich wanted to tell her things he hadn't told anyone, not even Amber.

The hinges on his own box were rusty. He had to move his jaw back and forth a few times to work them loose. "My team was on the trail of a seriously bad dude overseas. He'd slipped us for days, but we were closing in, and Fitz pushed us to keep going. We'd been outside the wire for days, way over the time we were supposed to be out, but..." So much was classified, but the larger fact was they couldn't let a big target slip through their fingers.

The day had been hot. So bright even their eye pro barely dimmed the sunlight. The memory was all white light and hazy glare. "Our convoy hit an IED that disabled the lead vehicle. Barnes and I climbed out to assess the damage. Fitz and another guy, Caesar, did the same." He could still smell the smoke and accelerants, could still feel the crawling sensation down his back as danger and death breathed nearby. "They came from everywhere. All sides. Firing. I took a bullet to the shoulder between a gap in my plates. Web was in the back and got hit over and over in the leg. Caesar, too. But Fitz…" Rich shook his head and pulled in clean, crisp air that wasn't tinged with blood or smoke.

Dana wrapped her hands around his arm, comforting him this time. "You don't have to—"

"I have to." He'd made the first incision, now the wound had to air. If he sealed it again with the words inside, the infection might kill him. "They must have known Fitz was our commander. They dragged him into the truck, kept us away with cover fire, and they tortured him." Screams like that weren't human. They were animal. Primal. Unforgettable. "There was nothing we could do. We were all in bad shape, wounded." *Desperate. Helpless. Pinned down.*

He'd been told another patrol intervened, but he couldn't remember anything after the insurgents tossed Fitz's mangled body from the back of the truck. Nothing until he woke up after surgery to a repaired shoulder and a wrecked mind. He'd never be the same again.

Much like Dana had found her identity shattered by a past she'd never imagined, he, too, had been changed by circumstances beyond his control.

"That's how I know you can still be you." His voice was a harsh whisper. "Because if you can't be who God made you to be, then I can never be who He made me to be." Whoever that was.

Dana held her breath, then lifted her head to look at him.

Their noses brushed.

She froze.

Rich stopped breathing.

This woman.

This woman with her breath warm against his lips

as hers parted, only an inch away. Somehow he knew if he made contact, he'd find himself again.

His eyes slipped shut. The outside world hardly registered. He could only feel the warmth of her breath mixed with his. There was only her. Only this moment.

The only peace he'd felt in more years than he could count.

Tilting his head slightly, he let his lips graze hers. The shock of emotion after so many years ripped through him with physical pain.

Dana's grip on his arms tightened, and Rich let his lips find hers again.

This time, he surrendered.

FOURTEEN

Dana sank into the kiss. For the first time in days, nothing else mattered. The spinning chaos, the lingering questions about her identity and how to prove her innocence… All of it faded into a peace she'd never known before. Peace that quieted her mind but thrummed in her heart. This was sheer emotion. For the first time in her life, she let herself truly feel.

It lifted the essence of who she was to the surface. Without a career, without a care in the world, Dana was simply herself. It didn't matter whom she'd been in the past or whom she would be in the future, because none of it would change Rich's thoughts and feelings. He only wanted her to be who she was right now.

Right now. When her life was a hurricane of uncertainty. When her mother was in danger. When death could be lurking around any corner.

Reality rushed between them, colder than the December air. They couldn't do this. She couldn't commit a part of her heart to any man when none of her life was her own.

When tomorrow could put him between her and whoever seemed to want her, dead or alive.

It took more willpower than she'd ever known she possessed, but Dana dipped her chin, parting their lips but slipping her forehead against his cheek. "Rich..."

"I know." He didn't pull away any farther than she had.

They hovered for the moment, in their own space, apart from the world. It would be so easy to stay here and pretend there was no danger. To pretend they could be a normal couple without the baggage of his past, the weight of her career and the threat of death around them.

Finally, he eased away, though he seemed reluctant to let her go.

Dana could appreciate the hesitation. It bored into her, as well.

Exhaling loudly, Rich drew her against his chest briefly, then released her. "Now isn't the time for either of us. Once all of this is over and you're back in your job, can we agree we have a lot of talking to do?"

Once you're back in your job. In Atlanta. Her entire life revolved around her career. Helping others...it was her calling. What she did. What she'd trained for. Who she wanted to be. She couldn't turn her back on it. Her job was half the reason they were on this crazy run. Not only to save her physical life, but to preserve her identity as a marshal, as well.

Whereas his life was built around the retreat center in North Carolina. It was a noble thing. Something he needed in order to continue to heal and to help others heal. She couldn't ask him to walk away for a relationship with the kind of woman who would always be needed on the job. Criminals didn't rest, and the danger to protect witnesses never slept.

The truth twisted her stomach until it ached. She sat up straight, braced her hands against the rough wood of the dock and shifted a few inches away from him. "There's nothing to talk about. We can't do this. Our lives are in two different places."

There had to be a way to sever this thing between them, to let it die a natural death without wrecking both their hearts.

Dana knew how. "We're not living in the real world right now. Everything is heightened. This could all just be a reaction to almost dying more than once. To being out here, where the world isn't digging in. Where we need each other right now, but not…" *But not forever.* It was the half-truth Dana had created to protect them, and she couldn't even bring herself to say it.

His lips drew together into a tight line, and he stared over her shoulder at something farther up the river. "You're right." He reached to his other side, handed her the metal box and stood. Looking down at her, he said, "Because it's all about the job. It will always be all about the job. It's what we live for, right?" His voice was hard, laced with anger and something else, something Dana couldn't identify.

It wrung her emotions, the pain swift and sharp, but if she caved to her feelings now, it would only hurt worse later.

Rich turned and walked away, his stride purposeful, his posture straight.

He had to understand that without her work, she had nothing to stand for. Beyond stopping whoever was out to get her, wasn't this all about her job? Proving she hadn't lied so her superiors wouldn't revoke her security clearances? Returning her life to normal?

As Rich disappeared into the shadows along the tall hedges separating the yard from the river, she wasn't sure of anything any longer.

That was the entire reason she had to free herself from the lies about her past and the men trying to destroy her future. Because she was in danger of giving her heart to a man whose past wouldn't let him accept it.

Of losing herself in a way she could never get back.

"Did you really do that?" Dana settled her coffee mug on the wood-plank kitchen table and stared at Emily Webster. She'd met a lot of fascinating women in her line of work, but some of Emily's stories had even Dana's head struggling to wrap around them.

Boy, did she need something to wrap her head around besides Rich and his kiss.

She also needed the coffee, because stuffed tigers, death threats and her roiling emotions had made her very familiar with the night sounds of the Webster home.

"I really did." Emily reached back and tightened her blond ponytail. "Don't let Corey get wind of the risk I took on that mission, though. It happened before I met him, and I've never told him the story. He likes to pretend he's got it all together and he doesn't worry about me when I fly, but it's a front. He frets like an old grandma." She stretched out her foot and pointed to her running shoe. "I track my runs with GPS when I'm training, but Corey has the app on his phone, too. If he gets to worrying that I've been hit by a car or taken a header into a hole somewhere, he looks to make sure I haven't fallen into a time warp. When he was out of the country once, he followed one of my races on his phone. It's kind of sweet."

Dana chuckled. Her interactions with Corey Webster had left a favorable impression of the former soldier with a slight limp. He seemed like a nice guy. "Sometimes it's good if they know what it feels like to worry." Not that she spoke from any sort of relationship experience.

Not that she ever would.

"Okay, what's the look for?" Emily stood, grabbed the coffee carafe and refilled their cups. "We were laughing, but now you look like you live in a garbage can on Sesame Street."

"It's nothing." Dana tipped her head toward her filled mug. "Thanks. It will be a wonder if I ever sleep again with all of the caffeine I've consumed this week."

"There's a real danger there."

"*Danger* is a funny word." Because it could apply to caffeine, killers…and kisses.

Sliding into her chair, Emily shoved a plate of homemade gingersnaps toward Dana. "You know, I haven't asked a lot of questions about why you need to hide. Knowing Rich, I'm certain there's a good reason. Not going to lie, though. I'm definitely curious."

Dana liked Emily more every second. She seemed like the kind of person who formed instant lifetime friendships, the kind who didn't hide behind a mask or let propriety stand in her way. "You're not nosy at all, are you?" She let a smile temper the words.

Emily grinned as she held up a cookie and prepared to take a bite. "Not a bit."

"The short version is my parents aren't who I

thought they were, which led to WitSec thinking I lied in order to obtain my security clearance."

Wincing, Emily set her cookie down and brushed the crumbs onto her plate. "Ooh. They really don't like that. Lying is worse than anything you could actually be lying about."

"Exactly. So I'm on leave until I can prove I told the truth as I knew it. But it gets worse. It seems someone wants me dead. I'm pretty sure it's related to the identity of my birth parents, but I don't have concrete proof yet." Dana twisted her mug between her hands, letting the warmth push away some of the cold she'd felt deep inside since Rich left her on the dock the night before. "My mom gave me a box that was supposed to give me answers, but it only contained legal documents and a picture."

"Did it help?"

"The picture did, in a way, but it still doesn't do anything to restore my job. This is so hard. I protect people in situations like this. I don't live these situations myself. I don't need protecting myself, but my teammates think differently, so I have Rich as a bodyguard."

"I can think of worse bodyguards. He's a good man. He's been through a lot more than most men could handle, but he's definitely one of the good ones."

"He is." Truly. Which made everything harder. Unfortunately, her heart was involved. Maybe she'd developed some sort of hero crush.

Dana sighed. Who was she trying to kid here? Everything inside her knew this was so much *more* than a superficial infatuation. This was a connection with another person like she'd never experienced before.

"The lady blushes." Emily laughed quietly. "So you noticed those dreamy gray eyes of his?"

"You noticed his eyes? You're an old married lady."

"I didn't say I was *attracted* to him. I said he had amazing eyes. Even Corey says so, but you can never tell him I told you." She smiled again. "So nothing in the box helped? No clues?"

Dana laid out the story of the box but left out who her real parents were. The world would look at her differently if they knew she was the daughter of notorious criminals.

"So you are your job, huh?" There was a light of understanding in Emily's eyes that nearly brought tears to Dana's.

She nodded. "It's all I've done my entire adult life. It was all I ever wanted to do. Other kids played school or wanted to be firefighters. I always wanted to be a part of WitSec. I have no idea what started it." Maybe something deep inside her had known all along she was hiding, that her identity was tainted. Rich talked about God and a story. Maybe God used her subconscious to give her sympathy for other souls struggling with who they pretended to be.

"Hmm." Emily eyed the cookies, then picked up a crumb and popped it into her mouth. "Ever been in love?"

Dana flinched. This was getting way too personal after last night's kiss. "Only with the job."

"Lot of danger there, you know." Emily crossed her arms and sat back in the wooden spindled chair. "Jobs are temporary. You might stay at one for decades, but it's still temporary. If you think about it, everything is temporary. Even life."

"Kind of fatalistic, isn't it?" If everything was temporary, then why bother trying to do anything? Might as well sit at home and eat potato chips until you died.

"It's kind of freeing, actually."

"How so?"

"All I ever wanted to be was a combat helicopter pilot. There was a time when that would have been impossible. Women could fly, but only in support. There were some trailblazers who made a way for us, and I was blessed to meet one of them when I was at Fort Campbell. She probably saved my life."

"Saved your life? You went down on a mission?"

"Metaphorically speaking. Dana, I was like you. I had the job I'd dreamed about and fought for. I wore it across my chest literally and symbolically. I didn't need anything else. I lived and breathed the job. When I wasn't flying, I was studying how to fly better or I was hanging out with other pilots. Being a pilot was literally everything."

"Nothing wrong with that. It's how you get to be the best."

Emily's smile was small and maybe a bit sad. "You lose your life in the process."

"No. You live the job."

"Until you lose the job. Then what have you got? I got a concussion once, unrelated to work. Stupid incident, really. I couldn't fly. I was totally lost. I mean, it was temporary, but it completely messed with my head. I was headed for a pretty good downward spiral, because who was I if I couldn't fly?"

"Like me."

"Exactly. That's when I met this other pilot. She was one of the first women to fly in combat. She fought for every assignment, every school, every mission. Women like her are the reason women like me get to fly. The thing is, she met a man. Got married. Had children. Walked away from the job."

"Wait. What?" *How?* How did a woman who'd literally been a pioneer walk away from the job she'd fought so hard to attain?

"Having a family was more important. Love was more important. What God had planned for her was more important. She's the one who got my head on straight. A job is a job. It's not who you are, it's something you do. You're blessed with a chance to figure out who you are, because listening to you talk, I'm not sure you've ever known who Dana Santiago is." She aimed her index finger at Dana. "Don't tell me she's a top-tier deputy marshal. That's exactly the opposite of what I'm saying."

"But she is." The conversation ought to make her angry, but Dana was too numb. So much had hit her, she'd lost the ability to feel.

"I met Corey two days after that conversation. If the other pilot hadn't talked sense into me, I'd be convinced I was totally happy as a career pilot while being seriously miserable. Problem is, I probably wouldn't even realize it."

"How is your marking your identity by a relationship different than marking it by your career?"

"Two reasons." Leaning her forearm on the table, Emily held up two fingers. "First, there are multiple facets to who I am, and soon I'll add more. I'm hoping *mom* comes soon, but that's in God's hands." She swiped at invisible crumbs, then looked up with a deep breath. "Second, I didn't say my *main* identity was in my marriage. It's in Jesus."

"I know." She'd been raised in church, prayed, had been a Christian as long as she could remember. So why did everything Rich and Emily said sound foreign?

"Do you really *know*?"

Now the hackles did go up. Nobody got to question her relationship with Jesus.

Emily raised her hand before Dana could speak. "I'm only saying you might have your identity placed in something now instead of something forever. You're who Jesus says you are, not who the world says." She sat back in her chair again. "Not to preach at you, but He didn't die for you because you're a deputy marshal or your parents are whoever. He died for you because you're you. Period."

Easy to say, but nowhere in the Bible did it read, *This is who you are, Dana*. Maybe finding out the truth needed to start with prayer. Real prayer. Not the one-sentence wonders she'd been tossing into the air lately.

The back door opened, and Corey walked in, followed by Rich. With them came a breath of frigid morning air and the faint scent of sawdust. When Rich's eyes found hers, Dana felt it in her toes.

Maybe praying ought to start now, before her emotions ripped apart her sanity.

FIFTEEN

Dana's emotionless expression drove a stake into Rich's newly beating heart.

When he'd first walked into the kitchen, she'd lit up the way he'd imagined she had last night when he'd kissed her, as though he was the only man in the world.

But then, ever so slowly, the impervious shell slipped into place, and she looked past him as though he was a stranger she hadn't kissed the night before.

It was almost more than he could bear.

Without a word to her or to Emily, he passed through the kitchen, the frustration he'd felt last night at her rebuff simmering to the surface. He might have a life story to write, but the theme was likely he would never be enough. He hadn't been vigilant enough to save Fitz, hadn't been strong enough to save Amber. He wasn't valuable enough to win Dana. Her job was bigger. It would *always* be bigger, which meant there would be no room for him in her life. He'd allowed himself a moment to dream about the future, and look what it had earned him.

More pain. It came wrapped up in a pretty Christmas package with a bow and everything, but the contents were nothing but heartache.

He walked straight out the front door, down the wide porch steps and onto the expansive front lawn. The snow-covered ground sloped gently to a narrow beach, where the St. Lawrence iced along the edges. Rich turned his face to the sky, to the sun that failed to warm his skin through the December air. *I thought this would be different, Lord. After what Web said, after I let myself open up, I thought…*

He'd thought he might have the capacity to fully live again. To take a step forward and write this story. He'd tried. He'd failed.

It hurt. Bad.

His eyes widened. Wait. *It hurt.*

Dana's rejection stung. Wounded his pride. Pinched his anger.

He felt something other than numb calm. Something other than emptiness.

Something other than grief.

"Dude, are you out here pouting?" Web's feet crunched in the snow beside Rich. "You walked straight through the kitchen without acknowledging Dana or my wife." He glided his hand through the air as if to indicate an airplane taking flight, then shoved his hands into the pockets of his jeans. "Kind of rude, if you ask me. And kind of not like you, considering there were fresh cookies on the table. Ginger cookies, even."

"You didn't bring me one?"

"Nope. I don't think you deserve one. I actually came to warn you Dana is probably right behind me. She was determined to find you." Web slapped him on the shoulder. "Tell her you're feeling things, man. Then fight for her. Go and make yourself a Christmas miracle." He sauntered to the side yard and disappeared around the house.

Feeling things? Had the man inhaled too much sawdust?

"Rich?"

His name in Dana's voice, and laced with concern, jolted electricity through the center of his chest. His eyes slipped shut. What if Web was right? What if he maybe sort of *did have feelings for* her?

What good would it do him?

"Yeah?" He wasn't trying to be standoffish or rude. It was literally the best he could do when her presence choked his air.

She appeared beside him in the same spot Web had just vacated, standing a respectful two feet away. "You're angry."

Rich stopped himself from inching closer to her. He crossed his arms and watched the river lap at ice on the shore. A denial would be simple. It would require one word that would hopefully end the discussion, but they'd both know it wasn't true. Especially after he'd acted like a bratty teenager when he'd walked away from her last night and just now in the kitchen.

He owed her the truth, not some lie he made up on the fly. They'd been through too much for him to disrespect her by hiding from her. "I'm a little angry. Upset might be a better word." He shook his head and finally dared to face her.

She wore her hair in one of those messy bun things like Amber had worn sometimes, a look he hadn't seen on Dana. It made her seem softer. A little more vulnerable with those wispy pieces around her neck and her cheeks. But it was her expression that got to him.

Her eyes held a sadness he hadn't seen before. She'd been all wild determination the past few days, punctuated by moments of doubt. Never had she succumbed to outright sadness. Not like this.

Sadness that had something to do with him. It sparked the slightest hope that maybe…

Maybe there was a chance she'd be able to build a new identity for herself. One outside her job. Maybe she felt something for him and could include him in her new life, even after she managed to clear up the misunderstanding with the government.

He couldn't push her, and he couldn't push himself. He wasn't even sure he trusted these feelings, they were so new and so different.

He'd loved Amber to the best of his ability as a broken man searching for a constant. He'd carry part of her with him forever, but Web was right. He had to continue living.

With Amber, he'd been grasping for safety, selfishly thinking he could be all she needed and she could somehow complete and heal him. This feeling with Dana was different. Less frantic. More intense. Deeper.

Overwhelming in a way that both scared and exhilarated him.

"I hurt you last night, and I'm sorry." Her hand reached for his elbow, hovered for a second, then fell to her thigh. "I don't know who I am anymore, and until I figure it out…until you figure you out, we'd be doomed for failure. I'm never a fan of failure, and I'm even less of a fan of failure when it comes to you."

She turned away and stared down at the river, same as he'd been doing when she showed up. "There's too much to think about and too many unknowns. I mean, what if we never figure out who's after me? What if this run for my life stretches on for months? Years? I've seen it too often in WitSec. Sometimes people have to forge whole new lives. Sooner or later, you have to go back to Mountain Springs. You can't hide with me forever or live your life looking over your shoulder. I won't ask you to."

If she did, what would he say? "I promise you this." Rich turned and stepped around so he faced her head-on, forcing his hands to keep to himself. "We will not let this go on and on. And…" Okay, so he knew the answer to the question she refused to ask. Knew it with a certainty he couldn't deny. "And I won't abandon you."

"You can't make that promise."

"I can do whatever I want. You told me I have my own life to live. Guess what? I get to live it the way I choose." He kept talking so she wouldn't find a sliver of silence in which to wedge a protest. "I helped Wyatt protect Jenna. I helped Sam protect Amy. I will not leave you, of all people, to defend yourself alone. I can't." Rich dug his teeth into his tongue. He'd said too much. Wyatt and Jenna, Sam and Amy… They'd fallen in love. They were now married. Had he shown her too much of his heart?

"Did you hear what you just said?" Dana stood taller, challenging him, meeting him nearly eye to eye. "You *protected* Jenna and Amy. Successfully. I don't know much about Jenna's story, but from what I've read in the reports, Sam and Amy are both alive today because of your actions." Something in her expression softened. "I don't know everything about Amber's murder, but I know you were with her. I know losing her wrecked you in ways I will never be able to imagine. When are you going to look at yourself and realize you are not a failure? If it was time for Amber's story to reach a conclusion, there was nothing you could have done to stop it."

You're still here. Amber was a part of your story, but not the whole story. Web's words circled, almost visible in the frigid air.

"You've had my back even though there's no reason for you to be here. If you hadn't come after me at the wedding, hadn't been with me at your house, at my apartment...then my story would be over." Her words fell to a whisper.

It was too much at once. First the emotions, now the idea he might be free from the guilt of Amber's death, truly free to...

He shook his head. The things Dana was saying... Somehow she'd shifted the focus from her life to his.

The need to be alone swamped him. There had to be a way to unpack everything he was feeling, everything God was saying, everything the people around him were insisting.

No, that was too abstract. He needed something analytical. Something tangible. A problem he could solve outside of himself.

As if he'd cued it, his cell phone vibrated. Rich pulled it from his pocket and glanced at the screen.

Isaiah. The preview on his lock screen might have just saved them both. Got the results back on the image you sent of the knife. It's from...

He handed the phone to Dana. "Isaiah knows who's after you. We can finally make a plan."

She blinked twice and her head jerked back, almost as if he'd slapped her.

Rich couldn't blame her. The change of subject had to come like a right hook.

"I… Okay." She took the phone and read the message. Her expression shifted, back to the one Rich recognized. The one blending training and capability, whether she felt it or not. "Let's move on this. I'm going to need computer access. We're also going to need backup, although with me cut off from my team, I'm not sure who it will be. You can call Isaiah. Ask him if there's any way for me to be involved in this legally. I want to be there at the end."

The longing to take her in his arms, to hold her close and shut out the world for one more second, was strong. They were about to go into battle. Who knew how it would end or if she'd walk away from him when it was over?

He kept his hands at his sides as Dana turned and headed toward the house.

It had to be this way. Otherwise, his emotions might kill him.

And the bad guys might kill Dana.

Dana settled her ice water onto the kitchen table and slid into her seat. The tremor in her hand said she'd pegged the caffeine meter. That was something she'd never have guessed would happen.

Around the table sat their makeshift war council. Emily sat to her left. Rich was to her right, and Web waited across from her. Dana slid the laptop Web had purchased for her earlier across the table and logged in. She'd spent the afternoon configuring the machine to mask her location. She'd also set up the necessary systems to anonymously access the dark web. It was her least favorite part of the job, trolling the depths of human depravity, but experience proved any answers she needed likely lived deep below the surface.

It was time to go to war, and Dana was the commander. They needed information in order to develop a strategy to end this madness, and a feat squarely in her technological wheelhouse. While Isaiah had assured Rich the feds were hard at work, there was no way she could continue to sit still.

"According to the intel Isaiah sent to Rich, the knife is handed out to higher-ups in the Hernandez cartel out of Venezuela." She tapped a few keys and pulled up the photo Rich had sent over from his phone. "The markings contain the family crest and are modified to indicate how many kills each assassin has. We're definitely dealing with professional hitters here."

"Who have yet to kill." Rich sat back in the chair and crossed his arms over his chest. "They earned those notches and, judging by the reaction of our friend at the restaurant when he knew I had his knife, there are consequences if they fail to carry out a hit. I'm not so sure what their end goal is." He shook his head and shifted in his seat.

He could cover all he wanted, but violence and death this close was eating away at him. One more reason to keep her distance.

"I'm not so sure, either." The incongruity of her continued existence had been looping in Dana's mind for days. When she'd tried to catch a nap while Web made his run for her laptop, the pieces locked into place. "If they wanted me dead, it would have happened at the wedding. They've had multiple opportunities since then, too."

Rich sat taller, and his fingers dug deeper into his biceps. Dana winced. After last night's kiss and his reaction to her putting the full stop on what was happening between them, there was no doubt he cared. Seeing her with a knife to her throat after what had happened to Amber...

She opened her mouth to apologize, then shut it again. She never should have put him in that position, but now wasn't the time to address it, not when they had witnesses who may or may not know the depths of his pain. She wanted to touch him, but reaching out might be perceived as a promise she couldn't keep. Part of what had kept her from sleeping this afternoon was Emily's story. *You might have your identity placed in something now instead of something forever.*

She tapped the keyboard and forced herself to focus. If they didn't find answers soon, her life might be more temporary than any of them imagined. Ignoring a knowing glance between Corey and Emily, Dana returned to her work. "A surface search won't give us anything, but the dark web may tell us what we need to know." She stopped and looked at the Websters. "Like I warned you, I had to make some tweaks to your system."

Corey leaned back in his chair but clunked forward again after he received a warning look from his wife. "Long as no black helicopters start circling overhead, I'm good."

"I'll vouch for you if law enforcement comes calling." She hesitated with her fingers on the keys. "You do realize I've never been traced, right?"

Rich's eyebrow arched and he shot her an amused look. "Pride goeth before a—"

"Not pride if it's true." She basked in his smile for only a second, then accessed the browser designed to take her into the deepest dregs of society. Drugs, weapons, hits for hire. Videos and images that would make most people recoil. This was her life, and she always came out of a dark search feeling like there weren't enough showers in the world. There were nights where sleep eluded her and she spent extra time with her Bible, trying to remind herself the truth would never change and God would win in the end.

It took longer than usual to locate and hack into a message board frequented by the cartel's members scattered around the globe. Without her typical bag of tricks, she had to resort to experience and what little she knew of the Hernandez cartel, but she made her way in. "Found it."

Like an overacted scene in a cheesy movie, everyone at the table leaned toward her. It would have been funny if the stakes weren't so high.

"What are we up against?" Of course, Rich was the first to ask.

Corey flexed his fingers as though prepared to do battle in his kitchen with whatever had popped up on the screen.

"I'm the target, but there's a no-kill order. It's a notch on their knives if they bring me in, same as if they marked a kill. We're talking high stakes. Valencio Hernandez wants me alive." She scrolled through the messages sent back and forth among the far-flung members of the cartel, searching for a *why*. There was none.

She sat back and let her gaze roam the three who watched her expectantly, trying to remember all she could about the Hernandez cartel. Because her team had never guarded any witnesses in hiding from them, there was little to recall. "Anyone have working knowledge of South American drug cartels?"

The men shook their heads, but Emily shifted her gaze to the side as though trying to remember something.

Dana waited, not wanting to interrupt the flow of memory. It was tough not to urge her to think faster. She dug her fingernails into her palms and fought to keep still.

"I can't tell you much or even how I know, but the unclassified part is there's a major player in northern South America who's looking to expand into arms dealing and human trafficking. Could be Hernandez."

"Then he'd either want to wipe out or absorb the competition." Rich clasped his hands on the table. "The easiest would be for them to join forces and create a syndicate, but if Marquez denied him because he doesn't want to share, then things could get ugly." He locked eyes with Dana. "Does the Marquez family have any other heirs? Because if you're the only one and Hernandez found out you exist…"

"I have no idea." She'd never considered there could be a brother or sister. Did she want there to be? Because if she had a sibling, they were in danger, as well. She switched browsers and went to Google. Some things were in the public domain. A quick search listed no other children. There was no hint Rachel and Jairo had ever had a single child. According to records about the Marquez family, Dana didn't exist.

She clicked back to the dark web. Had they searched for her? Put out any sort of hit on the Santiagos? The Marquezes were smart. They were bound to realize who'd taken their daughter, even if they didn't know where she'd gone.

There was nothing. No hits, no inquiries, no nothing. They really hadn't wanted her. Had no apparent concern for her whatsoever.

Despite their evil, the truth that her blood parents hadn't cared for her at all sliced through Dana's chest.

"Dana?" While Rich and Corey talked quietly, Emily watched her. "You okay?"

"Fine." She resumed her search. "It's good to have people to bounce ideas off. I usually work alone at this stage."

"Yeah, because that was what that face was about." Emily kept her voice low and offered a look saying she knew Dana was deflecting.

Frankly, she was tired of talking about her emotions when she didn't even know what to feel. All she wanted was her life back. She turned her attention back to the screen and did her best not to take in the worst of what she saw there. "Maybe the Hernandez cartel figured out I exist and their goal is to take out the Marquez successor. Jairo and Rachel aren't as young as they used to be. It's possible the cartel thinks they know I'm alive and are hiding me for my own safety and for the future of their organization."

"They want you as a bargaining chip." Rich broke away from his conversation with Corey and squared off to the table again. "Like you said, there's a no-kill.

The only reason they'd go through the trouble to keep you alive and risk transporting you to South America is if you were the leverage they needed to make Jairo and Rachel cave in."

"They think my parents care if I live or die. They got that one wrong." She couldn't keep the bitterness out of her voice. "There's no torque in that leverage."

An uncomfortable silence settled around the table.

Corey broke the tension. "Okay, we operate on the assumption you're the linchpin to their plan for global domination. Our first move has to be based off their next move, which is…?"

"Easy to find out." Dana offered her first genuine smile in what felt like years. "They're largely communicating on the dark web through a system of coded messages. It keeps the intel off their devices if they're taken into custody. It's tough to trace communications because they mask their locations and IP addresses. All we have to do is crack the code."

Corey linked his fingers and held them palm out in front of him. "Good thing for you, there's an intel expert in the house."

So that's what he'd done on Rich's Special Forces team. She made screenshots of the latest posts then printed them so Corey could check them out while she continued to comb through message boards.

Intense silence reigned before Rich looked across the table at Emily. "I feel useless."

She pushed away from the table. "We'll be the lackeys and make dinner. These two can clean up afterward."

Dana wrinkled her nose then smiled. If nothing else, she'd found a bit of the camaraderie she'd missed the past few days while cut off from her team and—

Her hand froze over the touch pad on the laptop.

Rich looked down at her. "Dana?"

She shook her head, eyes glued to the screen. A new message had popped into the message board. A photo of her mother getting out of Javi's truck and into a smaller SUV at the truck stop. The time stamp indicated it was the night of her flight.

There was a message addressed to Dana. We know you're watching. We know where your mother is. Come out of hiding, or it's her life instead of yours.

SIXTEEN

Whatever Dana was up to, Rich didn't like it.

He paced the narrow living room to the Christmas tree by the front window, pivoted on one heel and walked to the kitchen door. His footsteps creaked on the hardwood and set the ornaments on the tree into a dance.

Across the room near the entrance to the hall, Dana talked in low tones to Isaiah on Rich's phone. She'd shut him out since her face went white at the kitchen table, refusing to discuss what she'd seen.

She'd been too slow, though. Rich had spotted the picture before she closed the laptop. He knew her mother was involved.

While one hand held the phone tight to her ear, the other moved with jerky motions. Every once in a while, she'd glance over her shoulder to make sure Rich hadn't drawn close enough to hear, then she'd drop her voice lower. Whatever the plan was, she knew he was going to argue.

Which meant he had a pretty good idea of what was coming. Rich marched back to the Christmas tree and flicked the rotor on a small helicopter ornament.

For a couple who'd recently married, they had a lot of sentimental stuff on the tree. Photo frames and travel souvenirs weighed the branches among fat old-school Christmas tree lights.

When had he last decorated a tree? Oh, yeah. At Amber's parents' house not long before she died. Well, her family had decorated while he watched, heavy with anger and guilt after Fitz's death. It had seemed futile to celebrate. Futile to seek happiness in a violent world.

He should have helped her family, laughed with them, joined in the Christmas singing.

But he hadn't.

His mother had put her foot down this year and arrived at his house, driving over an hour to decorate his tree while he was on patrol. She'd insisted it was time to start living again.

Maybe she was right, but it was harder to do than it was to say.

Especially when Dana Santiago had scrambled everything about his carefully ordered world. She insisted on leaping into danger when she should be hiding. She spun up emotions he hadn't realized he still possessed. She made him want to dream.

Dreaming about the future was a highway to pain. In the end, all it got you was—

The room grew silent. Dana was no longer speaking. Rich stalked back to the kitchen door, steeling himself for whatever bomb she was about to drop.

She stared at the phone, her profile toward him. Her index finger tapped the back of the device, then she squared her shoulders and faced him.

Ready for battle.

She extended the phone and waited for him to draw near.

Rich accepted the device, careful not to touch her. If he did, he'd lose all restraint and pull her into his arms. He hoped he was wrong about the lengths she would go to restore her job and protect her mother. "Well?"

"I've been reinstated for this mission. It's probationary due to extenuating circumstances." Her resolute expression chilled Rich straight through.

His grip tightened on the phone. "Dana, you can't do this." *Extenuating circumstances* could only mean one thing. She was the only option they had to bring down two notorious crime families. They were willing to sacrifice her as a means to their end.

But he was not going to allow her to put herself out there as bait. "All it takes is one trigger-happy rookie out to make a name for himself with the cartel, and there's a bullet flying in your direction." One he wouldn't be there to block.

Her gaze was steely. "They use knives."

"This isn't funny." Fear raged through him. She'd cracked the wall around his heart and now she wanted to walk into danger? He'd listened to Amber when she didn't want to hide, and it had signed her death warrant. He couldn't let Dana shut him out and die, as well.

She was bound to be able to read the sheer terror he fought hard to wrestle into submission. He'd once been a methodical, unshakable soldier. Yet here he was quaking at the thought of a mission he couldn't control. This was who he was now. A man who hesitated. Broke. Failed.

The granite wall of Dana's resolve crumbled. Her

lips drew down as her eyes filled with uncertainty. A softness at the edges hinted she felt the same emotions she'd unlocked in him.

Hope flooded Rich, but it ebbed when she drew her shoulders back and pulled herself to her full height. "I don't have a choice. They tailed my mother. They know where she is. If I don't respond within ten minutes, they'll kill her. I have my team behind me along with a task force across several agencies. I can do my job. I can save my mother." She held her breath then released it slowly, almost as though she had to plan her next sentence. "I know this is hard for you, but—"

"Don't." Rich's voice cracked under the strain. "You have no idea. You've never had someone you love die in your arms because you were too stupid, too arrogant, to insist they go into hiding. You've never had the blood of someone you love on your hands. I won't let it happen again."

Her head jerked back, and her feet followed a step. "You won't let *what* happen again?"

Had he...? Rich stopped breathing. Had he really dropped the *L* word to her?

Did he *L*-word her?

It didn't matter. Even if he did, love wouldn't stop what was coming. Dana's heart and mind weren't in a place to reciprocate, so there was no sense in pursuing the discussion. He dug deep, swamped his emotions and let his heart freeze. "I won't let another innocent person die on my watch."

A brief flicker of hurt flashed, then Dana nodded slowly. "According to Isaiah, this is the first clear shot the task force has had at higher-ups in the Hernandez cartel. They won't waste it, and neither will I. I'm not some innocent bystander, Rich. I'm a trained agent these scumbags made the mistake of putting into play. That makes all the difference." She started to turn but hesitated as though she thought he might cave and agree with her. When he didn't flinch, she walked out the door, headed toward the kitchen where her laptop waited for her to respond to killers who had the power to end her life.

Rich hit the door frame with the side of his fist and stomped back across the room, a caged animal trapped with rising panic. He had to keep her from moving forward. There had to be a way to put an end to this before she got herself killed.

He stopped by the tree and wanted to shake it until the ornaments fell off. Futile. All of it. Love, joy, future plans… They never lasted. Like Christmas, they came and went. That whole God and the book thing? It just meant Rich had no control.

He was tired of death and grief and being left behind in never-ending pain. As he turned to stalk the room again, the ornament on top of the tree wobbled. He instinctively reached to catch it, but it righted itself and stayed in place.

The topper wasn't a traditional star or angel. It was a hand-carved cross, probably Web's handiwork. A baby nestled at the base, and a wooden ribbon wound around the cross with a date from this past September carved into it.

Interesting. It wasn't the Websters' anniversary. They'd been married almost two years. Why would that date merit a place of honor on—?

Oh, no. The thing Web had stopped himself from saying in the workshop. About them losing something... *There's a future here. Future dreams. I'm going to be a dad someday, when God's ready. One way or another.*

The tight frown...the hesitation in Web's voice. They'd lost a baby. A child they'd planned for and dreamed for. A child they'd loved.

Rich's panic and grief evaporated. His heart seized for his battle buddy, a man who'd witnessed horror right alongside him and had endured a different kind of pain without him, one Rich couldn't imagine.

Yet a man who continued to dream. Who continued to live. Who'd suffered unspeakably with his wife and survived with the hope that life waited on the other side.

Rich was acting like he was the only person who'd ever grieved. Like he was the only one who hadn't been able to protect someone he loved. How self-centered could he be? In the shop, he'd blocked Web at every turn in the conversation, so focused on his issues that he couldn't see anyone else's. He'd missed the grief of his loved ones.

The floor creaked behind him. "You okay?"

Web. Like a good battle buddy, he'd known Rich needed someone by his side. Still, this wasn't entirely about him. He pointed at the cross. "I'm sorry. What happened?"

Web walked over and straightened the cross, letting his fingers rest on the base. "Em was three months along. We were just about to tell everyone, and one day..." He sniffed. "You and I, we know what it means to walk through the valley of the shadow of death, but, well, it's worse when your wife's in pain. Worse when there's nothing physical to fight and somehow you still lose."

"You said you're still going to try." To know wrenching heartache and to try again. It seemed impossible. Even more impossible than planning a future.

Web gave him a side-eyed perusal, then leaned closer. "I get it. You've seen awful things." His jaw clenched. "*We've* seen awful things. It makes no sense, but we have to trust the process. Trust God's telling the truth when He says He's planned all of our days and knows the end from the beginning. Trust there's a purpose, even when the purpose feels like…well, like it's going to kill us."

"I don't know if I can."

"Want to know what I've noticed?"

Rich shrugged.

"I look back on the hard times with Fitz and with Amber and with…with our baby, and I see where God set things and people in place to get us through, to make something new, even. That retreat you went on— you think it was an accident? God had that ready for you because He saw what was coming." He exhaled heavily. "I don't know why He allowed the bad things, but we live in a messed-up world where horrible stuff happens. What I do know is He set up ways to heal and ways to use those bad things for good if we'll let Him. It's part of Him writing down the story."

Again, Rich shrugged. Sounded like preaching to him. Still, if Web could believe it after all he'd been through, then perhaps anything was possible.

Web's low chuckle was out of place given the weight in the room. "Dana really has you off the rails, doesn't she?"

"What?"

"I've never seen you act like this. You're the rock.

Remember how many times you had to focus me when it was time to go full battle rattle?" Web crossed his arms. "You're different with Dana. It's kind of good to see you not thinking you have it all together."

No, it wasn't. It was awful.

"I know I don't have as much at stake as you do today, but don't count a battle brother out. And don't count out whatever God's doing. There's a purpose. Even Jesus suffered. He chose to. It totally threw His disciples off, but there was a really big reason."

Rich drummed his fingers on his thigh. A purpose. Jesus suffered.

He'd suffered so Rich wouldn't have to. What if Dana and Rich had to suffer so two cartels were wiped out and innocent people didn't die?

It was a huge purpose. He'd sworn to die defending his country if necessary, and Dana had likely taken a similar oath. Just because those oaths collided with his pain, that didn't mean they could turn back. Jesus hadn't. His suffering had saved countless millions for eternity.

Rich shifted his focus to where it needed to be. Not on himself. Not on the selfish man who focused on his own pain. He shifted it to God.

He surrendered. To whatever God called him to do. Even if he had to walk with Dana through the valley of the shadow of death.

Dana leaned forward and adjusted the vent in the truck, trying in vain to chase away the chill in the air. The cold had nothing to do with the nighttime temperature and everything to do with the distance between her and the man beside her. It had been icy since she walked out on him in Corey and Emily's living room to set up the meet with the cartel.

It seemed like he'd said he loved her.

Love was a new brand of insanity in this mess. Rich hadn't said much after, had simply walked into the kitchen and stepped into combat mode with the rest of their makeshift team. He'd been tense, although he hadn't argued the way she'd assumed he would. His silence was loud, speaking of fear and pain.

Pain she had inflicted and continued to inflict.

Outside the truck window, glimpses of the St. Lawrence River flashed in the moonlight between houses and trees as they headed toward Alexandria Bay. Agents from the nearest federal office were already there, waiting for the next step in a complicated plan. The task force was broad, made up of agents from the FBI to the DEA to the ATF. They wanted the Hernandez cartel taken down before they could solidify their toehold in the United States. Evidence said they already had. The question was where.

Dana was the key to the answer. If she turned herself over to them, they'd likely carry her straight to their headquarters. And if the Marquez family sent higher-ups to bargain for her, then there was a good chance this op would lead to the end of two cold-blooded killing families.

Given the questions about her past, Dana was shocked they hadn't sent a helicopter to whisk her off the Websters' island. That they'd agreed to her plan spoke volumes about the government's determination. Yet their insistence on being close by was a sharp indication they still weren't certain they trusted someone who'd supposedly lied on her background clearance.

She'd wanted to drive herself tonight, but Rich had insisted on playing chauffeur. Even though she'd shut him out completely, he still stood by her. "Why?"

"What was that?" He glanced her way, but only for an instant. She'd watched him earlier, and his eyes never stopped roving between the mirrors and the road in front of them.

Corey trailed them about a mile behind, a second set of eyes to alert them to danger.

For the immediate moment, though, her biggest problem was she'd spoken her thoughts about Rich out loud. "Nothing. It's not important."

He kneaded the steering wheel, then cranked the temperature dial into the red. "I made a decision."

"Okay?"

"You don't get to slam the door in my face." He didn't look at her, but his voice was resolute.

He'd fight her to the end.

No. He'd fight *for* her to the end.

The emotion behind his words rendered Dana speechless. It filled the truck and cut off her oxygen.

He kept talking. "We're both walking this road. We were both on the dock last night. We were both involved in that kiss. I was there just like you were."

"I know."

"Well, then you also know there was more to it than a minute of thoughtless, emotionless…" He waved his hand into the air as if she should be able to fill in the rest of the words.

She could. Their kiss, this thing running between them, it meant something to him. That made everything even harder. Dana could fight her emotions, but she was fairly certain she was no match for his.

Rich gripped the steering wheel again. "I don't want

to watch you do this." His voice was low, heavier than the tension in the truck.

"I don't want you to have to watch." Dana stared out the front window, watching the headlights of an approaching vehicle as they briefly illuminated the truck's interior. "You can't be a factor in my decisions. Not right now." Could he be a factor later? Their careers and lives lay in two different places. That hadn't changed, no matter how much her feelings had shifted.

"I know that, too. This is your story, and I have to trust it'll go the way it's meant to go."

There was the story thing again. The idea God knew the beginning and middle and end. That He'd allowed everything…even this.

"Dana, I'm telling you this. You're part of my story now, and I'm part of yours. When this is over and you're safe, you don't get to make all the decisions unilaterally. We'll talk. We'll make them together."

Oh, how she wanted to sink into the warmth and passion behind his declaration, but there were no decisions to make. Once she glued the pieces of her life back together, she'd return to climbing the ladder at WitSec. The job would take over again.

What if she didn't want it to? Could she, as Emily had suggested, have it all?

Rich kept talking. "At the moment, we need our heads in the game, not our hearts. You were right to walk away from me earlier, but not to keep me out of the loop. I'm with you until the end. If the feds kick me out, then I'm behind you out of their range. I'm good at being a ghost. I did it for years." He flicked the slightest of grins in her direction. "Even the cartel knows it."

Espectro. The ghost. The man who appeared out of nowhere and protected Dana.

"I'm not going anywhere." His low whisper wrapped her in warm electricity. He wasn't just talking about this mission.

But the mission was the focus right now, which meant switching this conversation to tactical matters that didn't involve either of their hearts. "If this goes the way it's been planned, two major criminal organizations will see the beginning of their end tomorrow."

Rich's thumb tapped the steering wheel. She could tell their game plan went against everything in him, everything he'd trained to do and every instinct he had as a protector. The situation had to trigger his guilt and his grief.

His shoulders tensed, but then he seemed to relax. "The feds really think they'll send the big guns to take care of a job like this? We've already got three of their men in jail in Oswego. According to Isaiah, they're silent."

"I'm a high-value target who's already proven tough to take. Hopefully, they're past the point of trusting their lieutenants to try and fail again. If they don't send the big fish…" She shrugged. If they didn't send high-ranking cartel members, then this was all in vain. "I may never get my life back."

Rich's phone rang, echoing loudly in the truck. He pulled it from the cup holder and passed it to her, but it stopped before she could glance at the screen. She thumbed it back to life. "It was Corey."

"Something's going down. This is a mission. He wouldn't mess around." Rich glanced into the rearview. "I've got headlights coming up fast."

Dana twisted in the seat to look out the back window. About a quarter of a mile back, a car approached at a reckless speed given the curves along the river. "You're sure it's not Corey?"

"Not driving like that." His voice held an edge. "Could be a teenager in a hurry to beat curfew since it's almost midnight." His tone held zero conviction.

Dana's heart picked up the pace along with the truck as Rich accelerated to put distance between them and the rapidly approaching vehicle.

Dana drew her lips between her teeth as the cab of the truck grew brighter from the approaching head-lights. "Definitely not Corey."

"No." Rich's grip on the wheel tightened, and he straightened in the seat. "Brace yourself."

Dana hardly had time to react. The truck lurched. Metal ground against metal as Rich fought to keep the truck on the road. If he lost control, they'd roll down the embankment into the river or careen off the other side into the trees.

The engine roared as he fed it more gas, putting distance between them and their pursuer. "They're going to take us out. We can't avoid it any longer."

Another impact from behind, harder this time, sent the phone from Dana's hand onto the floorboard. Her head jerked. Her neck screamed. The truck shimmied between white and yellow lines.

Another impact smashed the truck, slamming her head into the side window.

Glass shattered. Rich shouted. Dana screamed.

Then silence.

SEVENTEEN

The seat belt dug into Rich's chest. The airbag exploded, and powder dusted his mouth. Gagging, he gasped for air. Glass from his window littered the truck, and the headlights cut a crazy angle through the trees to the river several feet below them. "Dana?"

No answer.

Rich shook his head to clear the ringing pain and tried to pull away from the seat, but the belt had locked into position. He reached for her. *"Dana!"*

She slumped forward and to the side, motionless. Her head rested against the passenger window.

No. It wasn't supposed to happen like this. She was supposed to—

Dana moaned then slowly lifted her hands and pushed away from the door. "Okay. So seat belts hurt more than I thought they would." The words were slow but strong.

Thank You, Jesus. Rich breathed the quick prayer then fumbled the seat belt release and shoved out of the truck, racing for Dana's side of the vehicle.

On the road above him, two car doors slammed. Two unfamiliar male voices talked over one another.

They didn't have long.

The passenger door didn't budge with his first pull. It took a second, greater heave that nearly pitched him backward when the door jerked open.

He reached for Dana. "Can you move?"

"They're coming. Let's do this." She slid out of the truck slower than he'd have liked and wrapped her fingers into the back of his shirt. "You lead. My ears are ringing too loud from cracking my head. I can't hear anything."

Rich's jaw tensed. If she had a concussion, the whole plan had changed. Maybe they should make a run for it.

Dana shoved his back. "Get moving."

As much as his entire being screamed to protect her, she'd never forgive him if he called an audible and changed course this late in the game.

Rich tilted his head to listen. Tree limbs cracked closer, and voices grew louder. He gauged their direction then plunged into the underbrush to their right, away from the headlights, angling toward the river.

He moved as quickly as he dared, crunching snow-dusted leaves and breaking twigs too loudly under his feet, giving away their position, making it impossible to hide.

A flashlight caught them in its beam, and Dana stopped, her firm grip halting his forward momentum and pulling him back toward her.

"I would stop there if I were you, or I will put a bullet through both of you at the same time." The heavily accented voice came from the direction of the flashlight.

"No. You won't." The tension at his back released

as Dana let go and turned away from him, tearing him in two. "You need me alive. I've seen the directive. There's a no-kill order. Violate it, and you'll be the one facing a bullet." Her voice was louder now, likely more bravado than strength. "Speaking of bullets, since when did a gun come into the mix? I thought the Hernandez cartel only played with knives."

Rich turned, praying their eyes were focused on Dana and her trash talk. He was careful to stay behind her yet ready to strike. If this went sideways, he'd have to shove her out of the way and draw quickly. His skin burned hot with fear for her life, and his hand trembled in a way it never had before. If he had to fire, he could only hope the shot didn't go wild.

This was too much like Amber's murder. Danger had invaded the personal space of the woman he loved, and he was helpless to protect her.

Cold metal pricked the back of his neck. A second voice spoke. "We like our knives, but *Espectro* has made life difficult." The prick deepened, and a warm trickle ran down the back of Rich's neck. "He requires a different method."

Rich held his body rigid. If he didn't, they could kill Dana and him in an instant.

Dana stepped away from Rich, her arms out to the sides. "Let him live and I'll go with you peacefully. It will make your lives easier now, and it will make your wallets fat later. If you kill him?" She tilted her head. "Well, if you kill him, then none of us will get out of this alive. I will fight you all the way to South America. Every step. We had a deal. My life for my mother's. You've already violated the terms by running us off the road and trying to take me before the time and place we agreed upon."

The pressure at Rich's neck eased, but not much. "As if we would let you reach a predetermined meeting location where your agents could be waiting." The words ground out, dripping with malice.

Dana couldn't do this. She couldn't give herself up to them. It was all wrong. They never should have plotted such a risky plan. Never.

What if they were wrong about the no-kill? She would be dead, and it would be his fault for not fighting with all of his strength. Not fighting for her the way he'd promised. His hand drifted toward his weapon, but the pressure at his neck increased, piercing deeper.

Blood snaked down his neck. "I can sever your spinal cord very quickly." The man sounded as though he'd take great pleasure in doing so.

Dana flinched and looked over her shoulder at him, her face shadowed. "No. I'm going with you." For the first time, her voice wavered.

"Enough talk. We move." The flashlight beam bobbed, and footsteps crunched closer.

Dana held up a hand. "Wait." She turned to Rich again, though he couldn't see her face in the glare of the flashlight behind her. "I'm sorry." She reached for him, letting her thumb brush his cheek.

She should have gone for the gun at his side instead.

The flashlight closed the distance, and Dana was jerked away from him, stumbling backward.

She didn't let them rattle her. "You let him go or I fight. That's the only way I walk willingly."

There was a pause, then an exchange in rapid Spanish.

The pressure at his neck released. A hand found his

pistol, and there was a skittering crunch as it landed somewhere in the woods behind him. His captor jerked Rich toward a tree and pulled his hands behind him around the bark, zip-tying his wrists firmly. Pain flamed through his body from his rehabbed shoulder.

He should fight. He could take them both. He could stop this from—

"You are the big hero." A swift, hard kick slammed into his ribs, exploding with pain as a shadow towered above him. "Yet you could not save her."

He doubled over, coughing and gasping for air. By the time he caught his breath, they were gone.

His chin dropped to his chest, the fight gone. His shoulder protested its unnatural position, and his ribs throbbed from the blow. If Dana died—

Footsteps ground into the leaves, coming from somewhere behind him and near the road. Cautious, stealthy, almost inaudible over the sound of his heart pounding. A figure circled him, weapon drawn, creeping closer. "They're gone?"

"They're gone. Kill the truck lights before someone calls the police."

Emily's shadow passed by and walked toward the truck. The sudden darkness matched the darkness in Rich's soul. Letting them take Dana had been harder than he'd imagined it would be. Too many echoes of the past.

"How's Web?" It had been his job to warn them when the bad guys showed up, to lend credibility to the ruse and to let them think they were winning.

"He's good. They ran him off the road about a mile back. Completely missed me driving behind him. He was the perfect little decoy." Emily laughed, but the sound was grim. They all knew the stakes. "We'll pick him up when we get out of here. How about you? That was a swift kick to the ribs."

Rich winced. "Sore, but I don't think he broke anything. It'll hurt worse tomorrow."

"So will the wreck." She holstered her pistol and sat back on her heels beside him, eye to eye, faintly illuminated by the moonlight. Someone would call the police soon and they needed to get out before the authorities kept them tied up at a station somewhere. Federal agents would work out the details with local authorities later, but they'd be in no hurry to do so tonight. "Do you know how hard it was not to pcg the guy holding a knife to your neck? I had a clean shot. It went against everything in my training to be passive."

"I know." His voice hung low and heavy. His entire military career had honed him into a warrior. Standing still, forcing himself to be helpless was not in his DNA. His heart pounded. His skin drew a cold sweat. If he couldn't wrestle down this panic, he was going to be sick. He focused on the pain in his side, trying to ground himself. "This had better work."

"I know it's hard, but you're dealing with a trained federal task force. They know what they're doing." Emily clicked on a pocket flashlight then slipped behind him and analyzed the zip ties. "Give me a sec to cut you out. Besides, the team knows exactly where she is. Those shoes are genius. Web once tracked one of my trail runs while he was stationed overseas. That GPS unit in the sole is practically indestructible. As long as they don't make her change clothes, that little device will lead them right to her location and the cartel's home base."

The bindings around Rich's wrists fell away, and he scrambled up as quickly as he could with his side throbbing. "Where's your car?"

"Slow down, cowboy. If we follow them too closely, we blow everything." Emily rested a hand on his shoulder and forced him to look at her in the dim reflection from her flashlight. Her expression was serious yet sympathetic. "Trust the plan. Better yet, trust God. This is going to work."

The door clicked shut, and a key turned in the lock. Dana was alone.

She would count to sixty to give them time to move away from the door, then she'd free her hands from the plastic cuffs at her wrists and her eyes from the blindfold they'd used to keep her in the dark. She ticked off the seconds. *One...two...three...*

Sure, federal agents and Rich would come for her, but she wasn't about to wait around bound and helpless.

Rich. This plan had to be gutting him. They'd taken a huge risk asking the joint task force to hang back while the bad guys took Dana, but it was the only way to make this work. If either cartel thought they were being watched by federal agents, they'd switch the plan and there would be no chance of ending their reigns permanently.

It had been hard for her, as well. Seeing him with a knife at his neck...

She shuddered. Since they'd blindfolded her, the image of him in the beam of a flashlight, centimeters from paralysis or death had been the only thing she could see. If he'd died, the blame would have been on her.

Hot nausea threatened to drive her to her knees. Simply imagining his death was enough to send her emotions into the abyss, but Rich had lived that horror. She could understand him more now, could understand in part what it must have been like to witness the death of someone he loved.

Of someone *she* loved. Dana's counting stuttered to a stop. Blindfolded and bound, she had to face what was in her heart.

There was no point in denying it any longer. Seeing Rich in danger had rushed truth into her soul. From the moment she'd met him, he'd been different, and she'd lied to herself about it. Told herself that his selflessness, his humor and his loyalty were all things she didn't deserve. All things he gave freely.

All things that had endeared him to her. Things she no longer wanted to live without.

They both had to survive this so she could confess the truth. But right now, she had to shift her focus from him to making this plan work. She had to fight. Her captors wouldn't expect her to be passive. If she was, it would raise suspicion.

She needed a battle plan in case things skidded out of control.

The count reset her focus. *Twenty-two...twenty-three...twenty-four...*

Dana inhaled deeply and tried to pinpoint her surroundings. New carpet, paint? Her eyebrows drew together. A construction site?

Wherever she was, it was likely a working front for their organization. They weren't concerned about her crying out, or they'd have gagged her as well as blind-folded her. Unless they'd hijacked someone's building, the Hernandez cartel was well entrenched in order to have a hideout in plain sight.

Forty...forty-one...forty-two...

Dana forced herself to sit still. It was difficult to gauge the size of the room, but if sound was an indicator, the space wasn't large. Her heart rate picked up. Claustrophobia had never been an issue, but being blind in a strange place changed things. Her mouth went dry.

Fifty-nine... "Sixty." The whisper of her voice in the room's stillness bolstered her enough to move.

Their first mistake had been zip-tying her hands in front of her. Dana pulled the blindfold from her eyes and glanced around the small space. Light filtered under the door and illuminated a room about six feet by eight feet. Drywall dust powdered the floor. Empty shelves ran from floor to ceiling. A supply closet, most likely.

Her wrists chafed from the thin plastic restraints, but a few seconds of pain would set her free. Raising her hands above her head, she winced inside as she brought them down toward her knees and spread her elbows. With a soft pop, the ties fell away.

She sagged with relief, rubbing her raw, red wrists. Raising her feet, she forced her knees apart as she brought them down, narrowly missing a loud thud with the ground. The zip ties around her ankles popped free.

Voices drifted in, too soft to discern words. It sounded like three, possibly four men. No women.

No way to know if there were only a handful or if a dozen more listened silently.

Oh, how she hated to fight blind.

Dana eased up to stand and inspected the space, but it was empty except for the built-in metal shelves. For the time being she was stuck, waiting for the federal task force to arrive. *Lord, don't let the battery in these running shoes give out.* If it did…

Nope. No worst-case scenarios. She didn't let her witnesses think that way, and she didn't let her team think that way. No way was she giving in to fear and frustration.

She slipped to the door, careful to be silent in case someone stood watch outside. Pressing her ear to the wood, she tried to make out the conversation.

The voices hummed in a low murmur, but the rapidity of the speech and the overlap of words indicated the discussion was heated. A mix of Spanish and English, based on the little she could make out.

"Keeping her alive is foolish!" A voice shouted in heavily accented English, then dropped lower, bringing only snatches of sentences to her. "Kill her now! If Jairo and Rachel dare… Kill them, as well. The risk is too great."

Enough. Dana inhaled deeply and clamped down on the icy fear threatening to swamp her.

Someone was coming for her, all right, and it wasn't just her team. The federal task force had expected lieutenants or higher in the organizations to show up, but not the top tier. Her birth parents were coming. Which was more frightening? Death? Or facing the killers who had birthed her yet hadn't wanted her?

What made them want to risk their lives and their empire now?

Nothing made sense. None of it needed to. Her life was nothing to these men, and they had no reason to keep her alive. She had to find a way to defend herself in case the team didn't show up in time.

She silently paced the small space, investigating every shelf. The metal was bolted too tightly for her to unscrew a piece of it by hand.

When they came for her, all she had was the element of surprise.

And training in hand-to-hand combat. Hopefully, it was enough.

The voices stopped. Footsteps. Some moved away from her. One set moved closer. A low, tuneless whistle drew nearer.

A key rasped into the lock.

Dana slipped to the side of the door, backed against the wall, and wrestled her beating heart and her shaking hands into submission.

This was her one shot. She would either survive the next ten seconds or...

The knob turned, and the door pushed open.

EIGHTEEN

"This is a terrible idea." Agent Collins, who sat in the SUV's driver's seat, had muttered the same phrase repeatedly since he and his partner had picked up Rich and Webster fifteen minutes earlier. He clearly wasn't happy about having two civilians on board, even if both were former Special Forces and more highly trained than his rookie self likely was.

Rich balled his fist and stared out the front window at the frigid morning. He wanted to punch the back of the young DEA agent's seat, but Web's knowing look stopped him. They'd only been allowed to ride along on this operation because Isaiah had stepped in. Apparently, he wielded more clout than Dana had let on. He probably also wanted someone he trusted near Dana. Isaiah had stayed behind with Emily to deal with the local police.

Collins muttered something about *cowboys* and *arrogance*.

Yeah? Well, that goes both ways, buddy.

They'd been issued a stern warning before they climbed into the vehicle. One interference and they'd find themselves on the side of the road. They were to remain in the building where the command center was being established and wait for Dana to be freed. No heroics.

Well, Rich couldn't promise he wouldn't get involved if Dana needed him.

He was about to start now. It was all he could do not to dump Collins on the side of the road. His deepest desire was to throw the guy out and floor the SUV to the office park where Dana was being held.

But he knew that wouldn't do any good. If there was a purpose to this, then they needed to see it through to God's end, not Rich's. From what he'd picked up from the conversation between Collins and his partner, multiple federal agencies were prepared to converge on an office park outside Albany, waiting for the call to take down their targets. As the lead intel vehicle, the agents in the front seat had been tasked with verifying Dana's location and the arrival of higher-ups from the Hernandez cartel and the Marquez family.

The female agent in the passenger seat held Web's phone, tracking the shoes. As they turned in the main drive of the office park, Agent Drummond lifted her head and peered out the front window. "I've lost the signal."

Rich leaned forward, the seat belt catching on bruised skin. They'd lost her. Because Hernandez's men had discovered the tracker? Or because they'd tossed her lifeless body into a pond?

Digging his fingers into his thigh, Rich fought horrific images. Collins was right about one thing. This entire plan had been a terrible idea. They never should have let Dana out of their sight. They never—

Web's elbow dug into Rich's side. "Trust."

Rich balled his fists. *Trust.* Trust Dana was safer in God's hands than in his. How? He was used to being in control and having eyes on the target, not lying back and waiting for someone else to be the protector. If he didn't have eyes on Dana...

Who was he kidding? He'd been right beside Amber, and she'd been poisoned before he even put together what was happening. Proximity meant nothing. Besides, he was unarmed. The agents had taken their cell phones and weapons before letting them ride along.

Web was telling him to trust. The man who'd lost a child and still believed God had a hand in his life.

It was hard to believe this was all going according to a plan he hadn't been briefed on and would never understand.

Agent Drummond looked over her shoulder at Rich with a mixture of warning and compassion, then glanced at the phone. "Most likely she's entered a building and the signal's blocked. She could be in an elevator or stairwell. Her last location is the tall building at the back of the park, so we're already on top of them. They have no room to slip past us." The words were directed at her partner, but Rich had no doubt they were meant for his ears.

He leaned forward between the seats, desperate for a glimpse of the building the agent had indicated. A block away, a brand-new five-story building with reflective windows stood watch over the area. It had the perfect vantage point. Anyone inside could see who entered and left the park. If Rich was in that building with a high-value target, he'd have a sniper at every compass point, ready to fire at the first sign of trouble.

It was likely Hernandez's men had done exactly that. "Approach is going to be difficult."

"You think?" Collins was all sarcasm and newly minted agent swagger. "We're working with the builder, and he's found a narrow blind spot where we can breach. The team will stage in the building next door under the guise of an electrical truck. We've got this. You observe."

Rich ground his teeth together.

Beside him, Web chuckled. Naturally. He'd always been the one on missions trying to lighten the mood and keep everybody loose. He'd definitely find Collins's arrogance amusing.

Rich sure didn't.

Agent Drummond rolled her eyes. Clearly, she was no Collins fan, either. "We'll be in the staging area, but we're not to be involved." She turned almost fully around in her seat and pegged Rich with a commanding stare. "*You* are not to be involved."

He forced himself to loosen his jaw, chafing under an order he honestly wasn't certain he could follow. "Yes, ma'am."

They cruised the office park, and Rich scanned the area. He couldn't act, but he could gather intel. A few of the buildings were occupied, with Christmas trees shining in lobby windows. As they turned onto the street near their target, a grounds crew eyed the vehicle, watching it go by as they chatted around a truck that held mowing equipment. "Lookouts. The lot hasn't been sodded. No need for the equipment."

"Yep." Agent Collins nodded. "That's why we're nothing more than a project manager and his crew, stopping by to check on construction." He tossed a quick wave to the men and eased around the curve, as nonchalant as a dude trying to wrap up business before the holidays. "We'll reel them in with the sweep."

They rolled up to the two-story building across a small alley from Dana's prison and parked next to an electrician's van. Everyone climbed out, slamming doors and talking loudly about blueprints and building codes.

Rich was careful to keep his head down when all he wanted was to burst through the doors with guns blazing to rescue the woman he loved. It took all of his training, along with Web's presence close behind him, to keep his feet moving in the right direction.

As he neared the door, the low rumble of a powerful engine and the hum of tires on pavement slowed his steps. In the reflection, a large SUV slipped by and pulled up to the five-story next door. Rich hesitated as the others entered before him, pretending to inspect the metal door frame as he watched the mirrored glass.

Web stopped beside him. "You seeing this?"

"Yeah." Rich pointed at a random spot on the glass, and Web leaned closer, pretending to discuss it.

In the reflection, two big guys who looked like they could take out half of the neighborhood with a hand clap exited the front of the vehicle. One took a position near the passenger doors, scanning the area.

Rich kept his posture loose to keep from betraying his anxiety. He must be nailing the whole nonchalant thing, because the guy eyed him for only a moment before he returned to his surveillance.

The second man opened the back door and ushered out a tall, slim man and a woman who moved with the elegance of a ballet dancer.

A woman who had Dana's chin and eyes.

His breath hitched. Jairo and Rachel Marquez had actually shown up? Did the feds see this?

Web opened the door. "We need to get inside. Now."

No. Something was about to go down. He wanted to be a part of the action. Needed to charge into—

"Now," his buddy commanded again.

Somehow, Web had matured into his voice of reason. Rich jerked open the door, trying to keep his hand steady and his gait nonchalant. He had one foot over the threshold when a series of pops rang out from next door.

He whipped toward the building as Jairo Marquez shouted an order. Goon Number One rushed toward the driver's door while Goon Number Two shoved Jairo and Rachel into the back seat of the vehicle.

More gunfire on the fifth floor. A window splintered but didn't break.

Then silence.

Heedless of the danger, Rich ran toward the gunfire with Web on his heels, like so many missions in the past.

Only this wasn't a mission. Dana was in that building.

And the silence screamed he might already be too late.

Dana jumped the last three stairs and flung herself beneath them onto the landing, straining to hear above the ringing in her ears. Two flights above her, men shouted. It would take them a few minutes to sort out the chaos and get their feet under them again. Their bulletproof vests might have saved their lives, but the pain she'd inflicted was all too real.

She'd bought herself a minute or two, but she

needed a place to hide and wait for the federal team to infiltrate the building. She had no intel on the threats surrounding her and no idea where the next danger hid. Waiting for rescue was her best option, especially since she'd angered Hernandez's men.

She'd managed to surprise her captor and render him unconscious with a blow to the chin and a choke-hold. Instead of the knife she'd expected, he carried a Glock 20. The ten-millimeter handgun was a lot of firepower for an underling in any organization. Her ears rang and her hands stung from the roar of the shots. The sniper and two guards had dropped, all wearing bulletproof vests, a clear indicator they were prepared to take the fight with Jairo and Rachel to the extreme. As soon as they gathered themselves after the force of the blows to their vests, they'd all be searching for her.

Below her, the seal on one of the heavy metal doors popped and footsteps slowly ascended the stairs. There was no way to tell if a friend or a foe headed her way.

She checked the magazine. Ten rounds left. The last thing she wanted to do was blast her way out of the building and risk taking a life unnecessarily. With a quick prayer that no sound would give away her position, she eased open the door to the third floor and slipped inside. She could hide in an office or find another closet or—

Her stomach dropped at the sight before her. Or she could give up now.

The third level was a wide-open floor plan with pillars spaced throughout as support. Floor-to-ceiling windows dominated three walls, pouring light into the room. She checked behind her. A nonworking elevator.

The stairwell door. The framework of four smaller offices waiting to be enclosed with Sheetrock.

There was literally no place to hide. Returning to the stairwell was too risky. Whoever was headed up the stairs could be right outside the door. She'd have to make do with what she had.

Faint shouts rose from the windows on her left. Lots of shouts.

A slight smile quirked her lips, and momentary relief took the edge off her tension. If she had to guess, the tracker had done its job and the team was already outside. With a quick glance at the stairwell door, she slipped close to the wall studs and peeked out the window.

Three stories below, teams of heavily armed federal agents surrounded an SUV. Two large men lay facedown on the ground, guarded by multiple agents. A man and a woman were on their knees, hands behind their backs as federal agents took them into custody.

Her heart seized. The ringing in her ears intensified, drowning out the sounds from below.

Jairo and Rachel Marquez.

Against all reasonable sanity, her birth parents had shown up for the meet. "Why?"

Cold steel dug into the base of her skull, stopping her next breath. "Because they wanted to look their family disgrace in the eye. Their reach is farther than you know. They've known where you were all along. With the knowledge of your position with the government leaked to our community, no one would trust them if they left you alive. They were losing their business to me." The voice was smooth, heavily accented and deadly with intent. "Now, hold your hands out to the sides. Grip the weapon loosely."

The pain escaped in a soft whimper and she obeyed without thought. She'd been prepared for physical blows, but her already wounded emotions cracked under what the man didn't say. Her birth parents wanted to look her in the eye when she died. They were prepared to sacrifice her for their business, and they'd planned to pull the trigger themselves.

Her throat tightened, and her eyes burned. The depth of betrayal, of apathy for her life. They hated her for who she'd become.

But they weren't her true parents. Her parents had sacrificed everything for her, had laid their lives on the line for her. So had Rich.

Her shoulder straightened. Her resolve firmed. She would not die today. She would not allow Rich or her mother to endure that kind of pain.

Dana pulled in two breaths. Her training had prepared her for a moment like this. "What now? Jairo and Rachel are already in custody. You're next." She lifted her arms slowly higher, calculating her next move.

Whoever this guy was, he'd made one fatal mistake.

He held his gun within reach of a woman who knew how to turn the tables.

Ducking away from the barrel, she whirled and stepped under the man's arm, throwing her hand up and over his. She twisted his arm down and away.

The gun fired into the floor.

Dana twisted harder and jerked his arm. With a cry, the man released the weapon. It fell at her feet.

She released him and stepped back to aim her pistol and solidify the upper hand in this fight.

He swung his foot, buckling her knee and stumbling her sideways. Before she could regain her balance, he swung again, his fist connecting with her chin in an explosion of stars and a roar of pain. Her pistol flew from her grip. She toppled backward into the window and slid to the floor, fighting to keep the darkness at bay. Fighting to stay alive.

There was some indication that the government had decided they weren't really serious about the

NINETEEN

At the sound of a gunshot two floors above, Rich abandoned all pretense of silence and took the stairs two at a time. His feet beat a rhythm. *Too late. Too late.*

From below in the stairwell, feet pounded, heading down. With the action outside as the federal team revealed itself to arrest Jairo and Rachel, it was clear Valencio Hernandez's crew had decided it was every man for himself.

At the third-floor landing, the sounds of a fight drew his feet to a stuttering halt. Forcing himself to slow down, Rich gripped the handle and gently eased the door open. He peeked into the small opening, praying Dana was alive and giving her captors a beating they'd never forget. Praying alternately that she was safely hidden where the bad guys couldn't find her.

His heart plummeted at the sight before him. Fear washed through his veins, threatening to weaken his knees and drop him to the floor beside his heart.

Dana was backed against the window, defenseless. A man stood above her with a pistol pointed unwaveringly at her chest.

His lungs wanted to roar. Every muscle in his body fought to be unleashed with animal ferocity, to propel him across the room and into the man who held Dana's life in his hands.

She was too far away. He'd tip his hand. The man would fire reflexively before Rich could reach him.

He was helpless, watching. *Just like Amber.*

No. He would not let her die. Not while he had breath in him. Dana believed in him, believed he was the kind of hero who could protect her. It was time to prove her right.

She shifted, and her eyes seemed to focus, landing on his. For a moment, she hesitated then shifted her gaze low to his right. Without changing her expression, she looked up at the man who stood over her. "You're Valencio Hernandez."

Rich forced himself to look away from the scene before him and followed the direction her gaze had led him. Just a few feet away, a large pistol lay in the drywall dust. A Glock 20, from the looks of it, powerful enough to stop a bear. Powerful enough to save Dana.

Valencio took one step back from Dana and leveled his aim. "Yes. Today, I win twice. Rather than strike a deal with Jairo and Rachel, I will take over. They are in custody, and I will be the one to personally bring an end to their lineage. This is a very good day, no?"

Rich edged farther into the room and let the door slip shut silently, waiting for Dana to speak again so her voice would mask the click of the lock. *Keep him talking.* He wrestled back the bloody images of what would happen if he moved too slowly, if he made a noise. Panic tinged the edges of his world, rattling his hands and weakening his joints. He had to stay focused. This was his one and only chance.

"I'd rethink killing me too quickly." Dana shifted slightly onto her left hip, wincing as she did. It was hard to tell if the pain she projected was real or was a ruse to keep Hernandez off balance.

"Yes?"

"Those federal agents taking my parents into custody are after you, too. You need a hostage if you want to get out."

Good move, Dana. Rich eased sideways, nearing the weapon, praying his heart wasn't beating as loudly as he thought it was. *Keep him guessing. Keep yourself alive. Lord, please keep her alive.* If she died in front of him...

Hernandez chuckled. "My men will never tell them I am here. They know my vengeance can reach them no matter where they run or seek protection. I already have a secure hiding place until the building is swept. I wait. Then I leave. So I lose a few men to prison. They are nothing to me. With the Marquez family beheaded and the heir dead, all of my obstacles are gone." He raised the pistol and leveled it at Dana's head.

Rich struggled for air and fought the instinct to cry out and rush the man. He glanced at the gun. So close.

With a slight smile, Dana braced her hand on the floor and looked straight at Rich. "There's one more obstacle. Now!"

She rolled to the side.

Rich dived for the pistol and came up to one knee, taking aim as Valencio Hernandez fired.

Hernandez's shot pierced the window where Dana had been seconds before.

Rich's bullet found its mark in the center of Hernandez's back. The power of the ten-millimeter bullet shoved him forward, and he crashed into the window then slid to the unfinished floor, moaning.

Rich rose slowly, keeping his weapon trained on the threat but glancing to assess Dana's condition.

She scrambled for Valencio's gun and retrieved it. She stood, weapon aimed squarely at center mass of the man on the floor. Her face was pale, streaked with drywall dust and tight with what might be suppressed anger or even pain, but she'd never looked better.

It took all Rich had not to blow the whole mission by crossing the room and pulling her close.

Dana didn't look his way. She held a laser focus on the man he'd downed. "He's whimpering like a child, but he'll be okay. He and his men were all wearing vests."

They'd expected a major confrontation and had been prepared for a battle. What they hadn't prepared for was one woman determined to fight for her country and one man determined to fight for her life, whatever the cost.

From the stairs, the sound of pounding feet echoed through the building. The federal team was headed in. Keeping one eye on Hernandez, Rich laid the pistol on the floor and stepped away from it to avoid confusion when the team entered. They'd expect Dana to be armed but not him.

He ventured another glance at her, and adrenaline kicked in. "You're hurt." Blood soaked the thigh of her jeans. Instinctively, he moved toward her.

She didn't look his way. "Stand still."

Right. When the team entered, he needed to be out

of the way and as nonthreatening as possible. But once this was over, he'd—

Men burst through the door in tactical gear, rifles and sidearms drawn, shouting orders. Choreographed chaos ensued as Dana gave a quick brief to the agent in charge and the attention shifted to Valencio Hernandez.

She didn't look in his direction. Her focus lay solely on the job. She'd apprehended the man behind the ruin in her life, had likely earned a permanent reinstatement, and was totally in her element. While he was clenching his fists to keep from striding across the room to pull her into his arms, she was oblivious to his presence.

Fine. As soon as he was cleared to do so, he'd leave her to do this work.

He'd be back, though. He'd fought for her this far, he'd fight for her still, until she saw he truly did love her and he wasn't going anywhere.

With a final nod, she handed her sidearm over to the agent in charge, then turned and scanned the room. Her eyes found his, and something in her face changed, softened. Without a glance at anyone else, Dana crossed the room and fell into Rich's arms.

He buried his face in her hair, the tension ebbing until he wasn't sure if he was holding her up or she was holding *him* up.

But that didn't matter.

What mattered was that it was over. Finished. She had everything she'd worked to achieve.

Yet she'd come to him.

TWENTY

The job didn't matter.

Dana sat on the Websters' couch and stared at the lights on their Christmas tree as they reflected in the dark picture window. Her thigh pounded where the emergency room had cleaned the graze and patched it up. Her head pounded from the adrenaline plunge and several hours of debriefing. And her heart pounded with the knowledge that had grown ever clearer as she told her story repeatedly to agents from each agency involved in the task force.

She was in love with Alex Richardson. More than she loved her job. More than she loved her own life. She loved Rich.

Nothing else mattered. She'd been firmly in her element, wrapping up the apprehension of Valencio Hernandez, and all she could think about was getting to him across the room. For the first time, the job was second. Even now, in the safety and warmth of this home, she felt restless and off balance, needing him beside her to set the world right.

Yet she had no idea where he was. After the brief moment she'd had in his arms, they'd been separated and whisked away to tell their separate stories. Emily had brought Dana back to the house to shower and clean up after her meetings. Isaiah had arrived and waited behind to bring Web and Rich back with him whenever they were done.

Pulling away from him had been more painful than the bullet that had grazed her thigh or the blow that had left a substantial bruise on her chin.

Emily sat on the couch next to Dana, extending a napkin-wrapped sandwich to Dana. "Eat something. I imagine the boys will show up eventually."

They should have been back by now. There was no way the feds had questioned Rich longer than Dana. As far as she knew, he had so much less to tell.

"So have you heard any news about your mom?" Emily tried again to hand her the sandwich. "Eat."

"Maybe in a few minutes. Thanks." The thought of food roiled her stomach. She was too tired. Too keyed up. Too…everything. "And Mom is fine. She's home now. As soon as we're done here, I'll head back home to see her." To hug her and to thank her for being the mother Rachel Marquez could never be. For sacrificing everything to give Dana a true, loving life. "Neither Jairo nor Rachel wants to see me."

She had no desire to see them, either, at least not at the moment. "They knew my parents had me, even knew where. They knew I was a federal agent and kept it quiet, probably thinking they could find a way to use me if they needed to. But once word leaked to the criminal community that Jairo and Rachel Marquez's daughter worked for the government, they started losing business. Hernandez leveraged that to manipulate them into a partnership, planning to double-cross them once they killed me. It's all so…twisted." The rest of the story wasn't worth telling. Isaiah had likely softened Hernandez's confession and the Marquezes' words, but even his edited version was harsh and bitter. Maybe someday she'd be able to look them in the eye, but today was not that day.

"I'm sorry." Emily reached across the table and laid a hand on Dana's forearm. "I can't imagine."

"It's about what I expected." Yet so much more vile than she'd ever imagined. That they could murder their own daughter.

A soft sound at the kitchen door behind Dana caught Emily's attention. She lifted her head and, with a quick nod, she squeezed Dana's hand and walked away.

Dana didn't have to ask why. The air had changed. Charged. Zipping along her spine with an excited warmth she only felt when Rich was near. She braced herself, pushed out of the chair and stood to face him. Facing him when she knew she loved him, when she finally acknowledged he had grasped her heart in his fist. He literally took her breath away.

He stood in the doorway, watching her with an uncertainty she hated, because he only hesitated when it came to her. Otherwise, he took complete charge of life. His gray eyes were dark with exhaustion, and several days' worth of beard roughened his cheek and jaw.

Yet somehow, inexplicably, he was more than he'd ever been. Larger than life and overwhelming. For a long moment, he simply stared at her, seeming to try to absorb the fact she really was alive. Then he cleared his throat and stepped into the room, stopping near the Christmas tree. He looked up at the cross at the top then back to her. "I think it's time we talked."

No, it wasn't. Everything she needed to say... It was all more than words. It was bigger than she could express with consonants and vowels. In one smooth motion, she closed the space between them, took his face in her hands and kissed him with everything inside her. All of the relief that he was alive, all of the emotion he'd unlocked in her heart, and all of the certainty that he was definitely the next chapter of her story.

His hands went to her shoulders, almost as though he was going to set her away, but then it seemed something in him broke. His arms slipped around her, holding her close, protecting her in the safest place she'd ever known.

When she broke away, it was only to bury her face in his neck, to take in the feeling that this was exactly where she wanted to be, that this was more than she'd ever dreamed. This was worth changing her entire life for. "I love you."

Rich's lips brushed her hair. "You're sure?" His voice was husky and rough. "Because..."

Because Rich wasn't a man who used the word *love* lightly. He'd loved Amber through death. He would love Dana until death...even the death to herself that meant life with Christ and with him. If she said the word, he'd expect all of her, the same as he'd give all of himself to her in return.

"I'm sure." She tilted her head to brush a kiss against the pulse in his neck. "I love you. Just...you." Nothing was coming out right. He was too close, swamping all of her planned speeches with his presence.

He pulled her possibly closer. "I love you, Dana. I can move to Atlanta. We can make this work."

"No."

He froze. "No?" The defeat in his voice…

She really was doing this all wrong. She pulled away and pressed her palms to his cheeks again, forcing him to look at her. "I love you. Not my job. The way I was living wasn't—well, it wasn't living. It was desperation. It was empty. I never decorated my apartment, because somewhere in my gut, I knew it wasn't forever. It wasn't the real end goal. I think I was always waiting for the thing that would make me care. Make me feel. Make me live. And that's—"

"Me." He finally smiled. He brushed her hair behind her ear, his eyes following the motion of his fingers. "Maybe you also love my cabin with its tasteful decor?"

"Maybe…" Dana laughed. She couldn't help it. Oh, man. She hoped this conversation was headed where she thought it was headed, because now that she knew what he meant to her, she never wanted to let him go. "I told Isaiah not to pursue my full reinstatement, because I'm resigning." She'd made the decision on the ride back to the house, Emily's words ringing in her ears. Making the job her life had narrowed her into a person who stopped living. Losing the job had opened her eyes to love, to Jesus, to family. She never wanted to go back again. "I'll find somewhere to work. I'll—"

"I know a guy who's looking for a cybersecurity genius for his private security company." His voice dropped to a whisper. "I also know a guy who's starting a nonprofit and could use a level head like yours working beside him."

"Would I like him?"

"I think you'd love him." His gaze dropped to her lips.

He was going to kiss her again. She'd let him. But not yet. Not until he knew exactly how serious she was. "You know…" Her voice came out hoarse with the emotion that seemed to rise up from her toes. "I'd need a place to live."

"There's no waiting period for a marriage license in North Carolina."

A slow smile crept onto Dana's lips. "So what are you saying, Richardson?"

"How about we rent a car…" He brushed a kiss across her forehead. "We pick up your mother." He brushed another across her nose. "And we drive to North Carolina as fast as the speed limit will allow so we can be home for Christmas." Then, finally, he brushed a kiss across her lips and hesitated. "I happen to have a killer Christmas tree in my tastefully decorated cabin."

"I haven't heard a question yet."

"Marry me, Santiago. Because I'm ready to read the next chapter."

"A girl needs a ring, you know."

"I may have stopped and bought one on the way back here, you know."

With another laugh, she kissed him, giving him the answer without words, trusting God that those would be put down in many more chapters to come.

* * * * *

*If you enjoyed this story,
look for these other books by Jodie Bailey
from Love Inspired Suspense:*

Canyon Standoff
Hidden Twin
Mistaken Twin

Dear Reader,

For years, God has brought me back to Psalm 139, particularly verse 16, about Him writing all of the days of our lives in a book. That has often brought me to my knees. God loves me—and you—so much that He doesn't just *think* about our lives… He writes them down. How intimate and personal!

With Rich and Dana's story, I wanted to deal with the hard truth that sometimes, horrible and unspeakable things happen. We wrestle with why. *Why didn't God stop it?* I've had many of those moments. Psalm 139 brings me comfort. He saw it all coming. He set people and circumstances in my path to get me through and to take care of me. I can say with confidence that some of the greatest suffering I have faced has led to my greatest joys in Him. I hope you can say the same.

My prayer is that you can see God in the hard times. That you can feel Him in the darkness. That you can feel His unfathomable love for you and see His hand at work. Oh, how badly I want that for you!

Thank you for coming on Rich and Dana's journey with me. I'd love to hear from you! You can drop by www.jodiebailey.com and see what's new, share your story or simply say hi.

Jodie Bailey

COMING NEXT MONTH FROM
Love Inspired Suspense

Available December 1, 2020

TRUE BLUE K-9 UNIT: BROOKLYN CHRISTMAS
True Blue K-9 Unit: Brooklyn
by Laura Scott and Maggie K. Black

K-9 officers face danger and find love in these two new holiday novellas. An officer and his furry partner protect a police tech specialist from a stalker who will do anything to get to her, and a K-9 cop and a former army corporal must work together to take down a drug-smuggling ring.

DEADLY AMISH REUNION
Amish Country Justice • by Dana R. Lynn

Jennie Beiler's husband was supposed to be dead, so she's shocked when he rescues her from an attacker. Although Luke has no memories of his *Englisch* wife, now his Amish hometown is their only safe haven from a vengeful fugitive.

CHRISTMAS PROTECTION DETAIL
by Terri Reed

When a call from a friend in trouble leads Nick Delaney and Deputy Kaitlin Lanz to a car crash that killed a single mother, they become the baby's protectors. But can they figure out why someone is after the child...and make sure they all live to see Christmas?

ALASKAN CHRISTMAS TARGET
by Sharon Dunn

With her face splashed across the news after she saves a little boy's life, Natasha Hale's witness protection cover is blown. Now she must rely on Alaska State Trooper Landon Defries to stay one step ahead of a Mafia boss if she hopes to survive the holidays and receive a new identity.

CHRISTMAS UP IN FLAMES
by Lisa Harris

Back in Timber Falls to investigate a string of arsons, fire inspector Claire Holiday plans to do her job and leave...until her B&B is set on fire while she's sleeping. Can she team up with firefighter Reid O'Callaghan—her secret son's father—to catch the serial arsonist before her life goes up in flames?

ARCTIC CHRISTMAS AMBUSH
by Sherri Shackelford

After discovering her mentor has been murdered, Kara Riley becomes the killer's next target—and her best chance at survival is Alaska State Trooper Shane Taylor. Trapped by a snowstorm, can they find the culprit before he corners Kara?

LOOK FOR THESE AND OTHER LOVE INSPIRED BOOKS WHEREVER BOOKS ARE SOLD, INCLUDING MOST BOOKSTORES, SUPERMARKETS, DISCOUNT STORES AND DRUGSTORES.

LISCNM1120

SPECIAL EXCERPT FROM

LOVE INSPIRED SUSPENSE

INSPIRATIONAL ROMANCE

*A deputy must protect a baby and
her new temporary guardian.*

Read on for a sneak preview of
Christmas Protection Detail *by Terri Reed,
available December 2020 from Love Inspired Suspense.*

"I'm going to find her." Nick Delaney shrugged off her hand. "She needs help."

"You're a civilian. Somebody trained to provide help needs to go," Deputy Kaitlin Lanz replied.

He flashed her one of his smiles, but it didn't dispel the anxiety in his eyes. "Then we can go together."

Digging his keys from his coat pocket, he held them out to her. "You can drive my Humvee. It's better equipped than yours."

"Fine." She plucked the keys from his hand.

"Come with me," Kaitlin said to Nick. Instead of immediately going out the door, Kaitlin stopped where the department's tactical gear was stored. She grabbed a duty belt and two flak vests. She tossed one to Nick. "Put that on."

Velcroing her vest in place, she grabbed her department-issue shearling jacket and put it on, covering her sweater. "Let's roll."

Once they were settled in the large SUV, Kaitlin fired up the engine and drove through town. Within moments, she turned onto the long winding road that led up the second-tallest mountain in the county. The bright headlights of the SUV cut through the darkness and bounced off the snow. They'd reached the summit near the gate of the estate when the SUV's headlights swung across the accident scene. A dark gray sedan with chains on the tires had slid off the road into a tree.

Nearby, a black SUV was parked at an angle and two men were dragging a female from the sedan's driver's seat. Kaitlin's hands gripped the steering wheel as she brought the vehicle to an abrupt halt.

Nick popped open his door and slid out.

"Wait!" Kaitlin yelled at him. The fine hairs at her nape quivered.

Were these men Good Samaritans? Or something far more sinister?

The men let go of the woman, letting her flop into the snow. Then both men swiveled to aim high-powered handguns at them.

"Take cover!" Kaitlin reached for the duty weapon at her side. She'd wanted Nick to appreciate her for the capable deputy she was, but not at the risk of his life.

Don't miss
Christmas Protection Detail *by Terri Reed,*
available wherever Love Inspired Suspense books
and ebooks are sold.

LoveInspired.com